# Changing Tides

# Endorsements

Sue Fairchild hits a home run with this tender novel about love lost. When Gabe Pechman's wife dies, he quickly learns that regret is an ugly bedfellow. Fairchild tells this story from a male protagonist's point of view and does a wonderful job bringing in a man's fear, self-imposed guilt, and desire. Interesting, moving, and emotional, Fairchild pings all our senses. This must-read debut novel touches your heart and soul and belongs on your nightstand stack of reading.
—**Cindy K. Sproles**, best-selling, award-winning author of *This is Where It Ends*

Grief is always a difficult subject to broach, but Fairchild does that beautifully. Through relatable and empathetic characters, Fairchild demonstrates that although sorrow may come for a season, when we open our hearts to renewal, a new chapter of life may be just around the corner.
—**Michelle S. Lazurek**, multi-genre, award-winning writer and author of *Who God Wants Me to Be*

A well-written and heart-warming story of a man who is frozen in his grief. An important read for anyone who has experienced the anguish of loss and is sapped by regret over what could have been. A compelling story of acceptance and hope. Looking forward to the next book!
—**Deb and Bruce Potts**, authors of *Love on Life Support*

*Changing Tides* is a well-written, faith-based novel with short chapters, making it easy for the newly bereaved who often have difficulty concentrating when reading. Sue

Fairchild highlights a widower's struggles during his first year of grief. Gabe has chosen to leave his job, his family, and his friends to live on the beach—something his wife always dreamed of doing. He finds himself questioning his faith and religious beliefs like most do when facing grief. As a clinician with over forty years of experience working with bereaved individuals, I can attest that Sue Fairchild has written a realistic and engaging story in *Changing Tides*.
—**Dr Sherry R Schachter**, PhD, FT, RN, President and Vice-Chair, National Widowers' Organization: *Connecting Men in Grief* and the Men's Grief Network, a project of the National Widowers' Organization, www.nationalwidowers.org

A gripping novel about healing from the deepest sort of pain ... the one you don't know how to reach. Sue Fairchild hits it out of the park with this one.
—**Robin Luftig**, author Ladies of the Fire series

In a culture that shies away from dealing with loss, Fairchild skillfully portrays through the eyes of widower Gabriel Pechman how coping with grief is a process. In *Changing Tides*, the reader watches how Gabriel consciously and unconsciously tries to escape his pain after the loss of his wife, Elle—all common experiences in grief. Yet, Fairchild also shows how, through God's grace, Gabriel is brought face-to-face with people to help him. This book is raw, sorrowful, and comforting, touching on some of the deepest pangs of grief. The author does an excellent job depicting how even in the darkest moments, God always provides hope.
—**Andrea Bear**, author of *Grieving Daughters Club*

# Changing Tides

## SUE A. FAIRCHILD

A Christian Company
ElkLakePublishingInc.com

# Copyright Notice

*Changing Tides*
First edition. Copyright © 2024 by Sue A. Fairchild. The information contained in this book is the intellectual property of Sue A. Fairchild and is governed by United States and International copyright laws. All rights reserved. No part of this publication, either text or image, may be used for any purpose other than personal use. Therefore, reproduction, modification, storage in a retrieval system, or retransmission, in any form or by any means, electronic, mechanical, or otherwise, for reasons other than personal use, except for brief quotations for reviews or articles and promotions, is strictly prohibited without prior written permission by the publisher.

This is a work of fiction. Names, characters, businesses, places, events, locales, and incidents are either the products of the author's imagination or used in a fictitious manner. Any resemblance to actual persons, living or dead, or actual events is purely coincidental.

Cover and Interior Design: Kelly Artieri, Deb Haggerty
Editor(s): Cristel Phelps, Deb Haggerty

PUBLISHED BY: Elk Lake Publishing, Inc., 35 Dogwood Drive, Plymouth, MA 02360, 2024

---

**Library Cataloging Data**
Names: Fairchild, Sue A. (Sue A. Fairchild)
*Changing Tides* / Sue A. Fairchild
248 p. 23cm × 15cm (9in × 6 in.)
ISBN-13: 9798891341517 (paperback) | 9798891341524 (trade paperback) | 9798891341531 (e-book)
Key Words: spousal grief; death of spouse; journey through loss; male protagonist; outer banks; beach living; coping with grief
Library of Congress Control Number: 2024932487 Fiction

# *Dedication*

To those who grieve, there is hope.

# Acknowledgments

When you start to write a book, you have an idea, some words come, and you write them down. Friends encourage you, until before you know, you've written a book. And when it's time to write these acknowledgments, if you have the right people in your life, there are too many to thank. But I'm going to try.

First and foremost, I want to thank God for providing this gift of writing and for showing me this story. What started in my head as an idea about how my own husband would deal with my untimely death transformed into a story about so much more with God's help. Without God, I would not have become a writer, and this book wouldn't be in your hands right now.

Thank you to my writer's group, the West Branch Christian Writers, for all their support, input, and love. Without you all, I would never have become a *good* writer.

Thank you to Tracy Cooper and Jill Thomas, who have been more than friends—they are sisters in Christ in this crazy writing life. I love you both so much—your input was invaluable in the making of this book. You have kept me on task with this book but also kept my mind focused on God in the process—a task more important than writing.

## Sue A. Fairchild

Thanks to my friends at Elk Lake Publishing. Years ago, I started working for ELP as an editor and have been blessed by the experience and growth in my own life as I learn from these professionals. When I submitted my proposal for this book, Deb Haggerty said it was "well written and intriguing"—a boost to my self-esteem. Then, when my awesome editor friend, Cristel Phelps, asked me to let her be my editor, I knew this book would be everything I hoped it would be. Thank you all so much. I'm blessed and honored to be in the Elk Lake family.

Finally, thanks to my husband, John. I hope you never ever have to experience the grief Gabe does in this book. I pray we will be together until the end of our days when we each slip away to glory on the same day and at the same time. I love you and am so blessed by your daily encouragement and love. Without you (and your job), I would probably not have this life of making my own hours, setting my own goals, and living the life God meant for me. But he gave me you in order to accomplish it all, and I'm so glad he did.

## Chapter One

Gabriel Pechman breathed deeply, wondering if he could suffocate himself with a pillow and blanket. He pushed his face deeper into the soft cushion, struggling to block the bits of bright sunlight streaming through his bedroom blinds.

*Why did I move to the beach again? There's so much sun here.*

He peeked one eye out of his cocoon to glare at the offending beam. His alarm went off, and he mashed the clock with his hand, then pulled the blanket up over his head once more.

*Six more days.*

He found it harder and harder to get out of bed as *that day* approached. To deal with the real world. To function. Maybe he could stay here today, wrapped tightly in his own little world, away from … people. He shifted further into the confines of the covers and closed his eyes.

A soft whine came from outside his bedroom door and then a scratch.

He pulled the covers tighter and snuggled deeper, blocking out his responsibilities. He had ten minutes before he needed to get going, and the warm cocoon of the bed offered Gabe the sanctuary he sought. He dozed and soon felt his wife's warm form next to him. He sighed. It had been a long time since they had stayed in bed together. He pushed his face into his pillow again, trying to block out the offending sunlight. Ellie stretched for him from her side of the bed, and he smiled as he extended his hand and caressed her cheek. Then he put his arm around her and pulled her close. She giggled—she was ticklish around the waist—and then snuggled into his neck. She reached her lips up for a kiss—

Something bumped against the bedroom door, dissipating the dream.

He threw off the covers and yelled, "Daisy, go lie down! I'll get up when I'm good and ready."

Reaching across the bed, he felt his wife's side—cold and empty, as it had been for almost a year now since she'd died of cancer. He fell back against his pillow as his chest tightened. When would he be able to rid himself of these vivid dreams about Ellie? He touched the spot on his neck Dream Ellie had nuzzled. He never wanted to forget her touch, so maybe the dreams could stay. But each time he dreamed about her, he felt the wound of her death open wider. If he couldn't escape the pain even during sleep, how would he ever?

*Time heals all wounds. What a bunch of crap.*

Another whine came from outside his bedroom door.

He could hear Ellie persuading him to get out of bed and deal with the dog. *She has to go out, babe.* And he'd not be able to fall back to sleep now anyway. His mind raced with things he needed to do, but his heart ached for his lost wife.

Pushing himself up, he ran his hand over his unkempt hair then his face, feeling the three-day stubble. He'd never let himself go without shaving even for one whole day before ... well, Ellie had liked him clean shaven. And she'd cut his hair. He'd tried to do it a couple of times since she'd died but had ended up looking like he'd been caught underneath a lawn mower each time. He sighed again. Time to face his responsibilities for the day.

Gabe pushed the covers away and snagged the half empty beer bottle sitting beside the bed. Taking a pull, he grimaced as the warm, flat beer swished around his mouth and down his throat. He could hear Ellie chiding him again.

*What are you, a frat boy? You're almost fifty. Go get some water.*

He wondered when her voice inside his head would lessen. She'd become so much a part of him during their twenty-year marriage he sometimes confused her voice inside his head with his own.

*I doubt water is going to do the trick these days, Elle.*

He shuffled to the bathroom before pulling on a T-shirt with "Monster Mash Dash 2015" starting to fade across the front. He hadn't run in a long time, and his flabby muscles told the tale. He'd taken up running a few years before Ellie's diagnosis. They had both been trying to be healthier people.

*Lot of good that did us.*

Maybe he'd try to get out sometime soon for a run. As he edged ever closer to fifty, he needed to think more about his health. Even though he wasn't sure how much it mattered, running had helped him keep the stress at bay. But now he didn't have much stress. Living at the beach took that all away.

So why didn't he feel relaxed and rejuvenated?

*Merchandising!* Gabe chuckled at the movie memory.

He thought again about running, then looked at his paunch in the mirror. Maybe not.

When he threw open the bedroom door, his fawn-speckled hound greeted him by snatching up her favorite toy and wiggling her butt.

"Yes, I know. Time for walkies." Gabe grabbed a pair of jeans lying on the floor, barely avoiding getting toppled by his overly excited pooch. He sniffed the pants, wondering how long it had been since he'd done the wash. Last week? Maybe something to put on the to do list for later today.

After tying his sneakers—not an easy task with an excited pup bumping into him every two seconds—he grabbed the dog's leash and nearly stumbled over her to the door. "Gees, give me a minute! You can't kill me if you want to go for the walk."

At the sound of her favorite word, the hound's butt went into overdrive, making snapping on her leash a monumental task. He pushed down his frustration.

*How did Ellie do this every day? If I had known I would be doing this alone, I wouldn't have agreed to another dog.* Yet, he had to admit the mutt had been a good companion for him and a reason to get out of bed every day. If he'd rejected this crazy dog from the beginning—yet another thing he'd agreed to for Ellie—would Gabe still even be here? There had been many days when Daisy's presence had given him the strength to go on.

There were also times when he wondered how a person could live a life with so much grief and not contemplate ending it. He thought back to the cushy pillow and how it could so easily be used for destruction instead of comfort.

He shook his head. No, he'd not consider taking his own life no matter how tough times got. He might have fallen away from God, but he didn't need a ticket straight to hell.

He remembered his debate with Ellie on the topic.

"You know, we can't prove people who commit suicide go to hell," Ellie had often said.

"No," he'd argued, "but we're supposed to obey the Lord and put our trust in him. If we take things into our own hands, isn't that turning our backs on him?"

"But he doesn't turn his back on *us* is the point."

The topic had been one of the few things they had not agreed upon. But Gabe's thoughts on the subject kept him surviving through difficult times and with two feet planted on earth—no matter how much he'd rather be with Ellie right now.

Daisy catapulted out the door the minute he opened the screen, and he attempted to rein her in. "You know the rules, kid. Let's not rip my arm off."

The pup thumped down the stairs ahead of him, while Gabe fought hard to stay upright.

*Daisy might help with the deed if she keeps this up. Would I go to heaven then?*

He brushed the thought away again as he looked at the dark interior of the business below his apartment, knowing Bill would be waiting for him inside soon. The quirky little coffee shop—Perks-A-Lot—was another thing that had kept him going. When he'd first moved to Avon, he'd been on the lookout for a place to live and work—things to keep him busy. Bill Brower's coffee shop and the apartment for rent upstairs had been the perfect fit. Bill had told him the place had been empty for almost a year, so Gabe had negotiated the rent down by offering to help in the coffee shop several times a week with reduced pay. Despite not liking coffee, or serving customers, he'd grown kind of fond of the place now as well as Bill, so he didn't want to be late.

"Let's go, Daisy. Get your business done so I can get to work."

Thirty minutes later, he walked with a now-less-excited Daisy back up the outside steps to his apartment. "I'm glad you're getting older. At least it doesn't take as much to wear you out these days."

Daisy's tongue lolled out the side of her mouth, making her look as if she smiled. Gabe felt a surge of happiness that he'd kept his end of the bargain with Ellie.

"When I die, you can't give Daisy back to the shelter. Promise," she'd begged him.

He'd reluctantly agreed—mainly because he'd grown fond of the mutt too. Now he felt proud he'd been able to keep the dog alive, but he knew Daisy missed Ellie almost as much as he did. When his wife died, Gabe had lined Daisy's bed with one of Ellie's old T-shirts. Daisy sometimes snuggled under it and moaned in her sleep. He wondered if dogs dreamed, and if so, if they had nightmares like he did. Maybe Daisy moaned because Gabe was not a very good dog parent.

When he unsnapped Daisy's leash, she ran for her water bowl and lapped the thing dry. He bent down to retrieve it after filling her other bowl with food. When he turned back with the full water bowl, Daisy was standing by the bowl but not eating. She looked at the bowl full of food and then at him.

"Oh, right. Sit." Daisy's butt hit the floor, and he bent down for the paw she automatically held out to shake. Then she licked his hand twice and turned to her bowl.

*Stupid routines.*

Checking the hour on his phone, he saw he'd missed several texts from his sister begging him to contact her. He hadn't touched base with her in a while but didn't want to talk. She'd want him to dig into his grief or go to counseling.

But he *was* dealing with his grief. He'd moved here to get away from it. That was dealing. And counseling was his sister's thing, not his. She'd been in counseling for every minor trauma since high school.

What he needed was to keep busy and push his former life from his mind. His mind would eventually heal and not see Ellie around every corner.

*Right?*

Glancing at the time again, he hurried to get ready. He changed his T-shirt and chugged a glass full of water after brushing his teeth and gargling with mouthwash. He didn't need Bill giving him the "alcohol is bad for you" lecture again. Then he grabbed a diet soda from the fridge and headed down the interior back stairway to the coffeehouse.

## Chapter Two

Gabe caught Bill engaging in his own morning vice—a sneaked cigarette out the half-open back door of the shop. When the older man saw Gabe, he took a quick last puff and stubbed the butt out on the doorjamb.

"You know Gladys is going to kill you if those cigarettes don't first," Gabe said.

Bill moved back into the shop, and Gabe could smell a mix of sea air and cigarette smoke wafting after him. Gabe followed as he moved into the kitchen.

Bill threw an apron at him. "Put that on, and we'll say our prayer."

"Do we have to?"

Bill was a devout Christian and began each morning in prayer, much to Gabe's dismay. It was the only time he prayed anymore.

"You know it's how we start our day here. Just close your eyes and pretend. God will do the rest." Bill grabbed Gabe's hand, then bowed his head. "Lord, thank you for another day in this place. I ask you will use us—both of us—to do your will. Bring those to our little shop that need guidance, a listening ear, and a good cup of coffee. We are so blessed by all you provide for us and ask you to continue to give us what we need and not just what we want. Thank you, Lord. We love you. We ask all this in Jesus's name. Amen."

Bill released Gabe's hand and began to wipe off the counter with a damp sponge. "See? Not so bad, right?"

Gabe decided to ignore his comment and went back to Bill's vice instead. "As fun as it would be to quit smoking your death sticks, I imagine."

At almost seventy, Bill was in decent health. Although Gabe had not known him for long, he knew the man walked every day—walked almost everywhere really—and that his wife Gladys kept a tight rein on his eating habits. Despite her best efforts, Bill's paunch had grown over the last few months—probably as a result of eating the sweet treats Gladys baked for customers. He wondered what God thought of how the old man abused the vessel he'd provided. But then Gabe remembered his own ever-softening muscles and chose not to bring up that little fact.

Gabe looked at the clock over the kitchen sink. "Could we have prayed for no customers instead, at least?"

Bill sniffed and returned to his chore, ignoring Gabe's chiding. "We've had a few customers already, but you know how Saturdays are. Kind of slow with everyone heading out of town." He turned to Gabe and frowned. "But I kind of need customers to stay afloat, ya know."

Gabe instantly felt bad for his comment but still had a love-hate relationship with Saturdays. On one hand, the shop was quiet because lots of people were leaving town. On the other hand, a lot of people would be arriving soon too. Most vacationers were a special breed of jerks. Something he'd never fully understood when he'd been a tourist himself. But after moving to Avon, North Carolina, he'd come to quickly realize how horribly most travelers behaved.

Bill smacked him on the back, breaking him from his reverie. "Gladys wants me to invite you to dinner tonight. She's making a crab boil."

Gabe shook his head. "No, thanks. I've got plans."

"To do what? Wallow in some beer and mistreat your dog?"

"I don't mistreat my dog."

"Hmpf. I notice you didn't deny the other part of my sentence. And you sure don't dote on that dog either. Poor thing up there by herself all day while you work two jobs." Bill eyed Gabe a minute before saying, "And speaking of vices … like how you drink yourself into a stupor every night. Do you even ever play with that beautiful pup?"

"She has a soft bed and two square meals a day plus the occasional treat. And I just walked her. She's fine." Gabe moved to the coffee maker and started a fresh pot. Bill's chiding rankled his nerves. He'd moved here—away from friends and family—to be alone and try to forget his grief. "And I don't drink myself into a stupor."

He didn't need some guy he barely knew adding to his issues. Sure, he drank almost every night, but he didn't drive anywhere and didn't get into fights or anything. What was the big deal?

He turned his attention back to the coffee maker. Even after six months of working here, he had to consult the little instruction sheet Bill had posted next to the machine. He preferred his caffeine with bubbles, not bitter like his soul.

"Well, that's good to know. But maybe I'll drop in on you sometime to assess the validity of that statement." Bill leaned against the counter while Gabe scowled at him and then continued scooping coffee grounds into a filter. "Have you had any breakfast?"

Gabe shook his head, and Bill turned to the fridge. "Let me whip you up an egg sandwich."

Bill offered quick and easy breakfast sandwiches along with a large selection of coffees in every flavor imaginable. Gladys also baked the pastries for the shop, which sold a lot more than the cooked stuff.

"You know I hate eggs."

Bill paused for a moment with a carton of eggs in his hand before turning back to the fridge and grabbing slices of bacon instead. "Okay, a bacon sandwich then. No one hates bacon."

Gabe couldn't disagree and left his friend do what he wanted to do. Grabbing the broom, he walked out of the coffee shop to the front porch and began sweeping up the accumulated sand. A useless task since sand particles gathered daily and fell into cracks of the wooden porch. Bill had often told him to leave it, that it gave the place a beachy feel, but Gabe needed to keep busy, and Saturdays were often slow.

As he turned to reenter the shop, a large, white Cadillac crunched into the driveway. He hurried back inside.

"Hattie. Incoming."

Bill wiped his hands down his apron, then through his thinning hair. "Battle stations."

## Chapter Three

"Here's hoping she's in a good mood today." He turned back to quickly finish Gabe's sandwich.

Hattie Mae Winston was a regular customer of Perks-A-Lot and the grande dame of the neighborhood—well, probably the whole town. According to Bill, she'd lived in Avon for the last thirty years and was probably close to ninety years old. No one had enough guts to ask her, and it was impolite to ask a lady her age anyway. She'd been a schoolteacher and had moved here with her husband in retirement.

Most days she had a sour attitude or, at least, an outspoken one. The last time she'd been in the shop, she'd said Gabe "won't hit a lick at a snake," which Bill told him later meant she thought he was lazy because he was working in a coffee shop at his age. She didn't know his story, but Gabe wondered if it would matter if she did.

The screen door swished open. A bedazzled pink cane entered first, followed by Hattie in the loudest pair of pink Bermuda shorts Gabe had ever seen. He turned away from the sight of her knobby knees to fiddle with the espresso machine.

Bill handed Gabe his bacon sandwich, then turned to address Hattie. "Hello, my dear. How are you today?"

Both men knew not to push the old woman as they did with other customers, asking what they wanted almost as soon as they entered the shop. Ms. Hattie Mae Winston—former Southern debutante and now Avon's most outspoken senior—couldn't be rushed.

She shuffled to the counter, the scent of lilies and powder wafting ahead of her. Her ruby red stained lips curved up into a smile—a good sign.

"Mornin' William. Gabriel. Gonna be hotter'n a goat's butt in a pepper patch out there today."

Bill glanced at Gabe before turning to the older woman and smiling back. "Yes, ma'am. No doubt—even though it's September, the heat still holds on. Fresh batch of tourists coming in today, though. Can't wait to see what the Lord brings our way."

Gabe considered the sandwich Bill had handed him. He must have used half the pack of bacon. Two thick slices of sourdough bread and a pound of butter encased the dripping meat.

*Yuck. Don't eat that, babe. Remember your cholesterol.*

Ellie's voice in his head echoed his own doubts. But he did like bacon.

Gabe shoved a corner of the sandwich into his mouth. The salty, greasy concoction mixed with the carb overload, and Gabe grimaced. Definitely too much butter. And messy. He looked around for a napkin. He'd have to have a chat with Bill about his sandwich-making skills.

As he wiped the grease from his face, Gabe heard Hattie say, "Smells like blueberries and bacon."

"Yes! Your smeller is still as sharp as always. I just made Gabe a bacon sandwich." Bill smiled his way, and Gabe gestured with the sandwich, attempting to smile despite his disgust. "Gladys baked up some blueberry scones and muffins too. We also have banana. What can I get you today? How about a bacon sandwich?"

*Don't let her eat that heart attack on sourdough, Gabe.*

Gabe shoved the sandwich onto a plate and pushed it away as his mind readied itself for service. Hattie didn't like to wait.

The old woman turned and shuffled to the one table in the shop.

Gabe sighed. If she sat, she stayed—at least for a while. He brushed another smear of butter from the corner of his mouth and assessed his attire. He wished he'd washed these jeans.

"You can start me with a cup of black coffee." She pointed one gnarled finger Gabe's way. "Don't go getting fancy on me, ya hear? No cream. No whipped ... whatever. Black."

"Yes, ma'am." Gabe turned to the coffee maker. "Just like every other day," he mumbled as he wondered how Southern she could be if she didn't take everything with a ton of sugar.

"What's that, dear?" Hattie called as she sank down into the shop's only padded chair. "You know my hearing ain't what it used to be."

Bill shot Gabe a stern look and said, "He's just talking to himself, Hattie. He's still getting used to how things run around here."

Hattie harrumphed, then pushed a stray gray curl back into the shellacked shell of hair atop her head. "After six months of living here, ya'd think he'd have caught on by now." She picked a speck of lint off her neon pink top.

Gabe brought the older lady her coffee in a mug that read *Beach, please* then turned to flee back to the kitchen. But Hattie grabbed his arm, preventing him from his goal.

"Come sit next to me, Gabriel, and let William run the place for a bit."

Gabe looked around, wondering if she saw other customers he didn't. With a forlorn look at his boss, he pulled up a chair and sat next to the woman.

She blew a bit on her coffee before taking a tentative sip and grimacing. "Lord a mercy. That'll put some hair on ya. How many scoops you put in this, son?"

Bill brought Gabe his sandwich on a plate along with a soda before saying, "He made it like I instructed, Hattie. Same today as every day."

Gabe eyed the heart attack on a plate. He didn't want to offend his boss by not eating it, especially when he was standing up for his coffee-making skills. Had he put too many scoops in this morning? He couldn't remember.

"We've made coffee the same way for over fifteen years, and you know it," Bill admonished the old woman now from behind the counter—a safe space to poke the bear. "Maybe your taste buds are off today."

Hattie glared at Bill, then turned back to Gabe. "Do you know what those tourists next to me did last night?"

"No, ma'am."

"They swam buck naked in their pool! Right where I could see." She took another sip of her coffee and grimaced again. "Get me some sugar, dear."

Gabe jumped up to grab the sugar and returned with two packets of sweetener.

Hattie looked at the yellow packets as if he were attempting to serve her arsenic. "*Sugar*, son. Not poison. The white packets. Four."

Gabe raised his eyebrows at Bill, then fetched the correct supplies. Maybe she was Southern after all. He sat and watched Hattie pour each packet into her black coffee, methodically stirring for several seconds between each one. After all four packets had been poured into the offending brew, she took another sip and sighed.

"So what did you do about the neighbors, Hattie?" Bill asked.

She lifted her chin and offered a satisfied smile. "Watched, of course." Gabe nearly choked and grabbed his soda to quell a potential cough. "It's not like they were trying to hide it. My house has a deck that looks right over the stupid pool, after all. They didn't think I could see, a course. Probably think I'm too old and my eyesight ain't the best in the dark, but that pool has lights under the water, ya know. Lights up everything clear as day. There's tree stumps in the Louisiana swamp with higher IQs than some of these tourists."

Bill guffawed, and Gabe suppressed a smile.

Hattie pointed to the sandwich. "Ya ain't gonna eat that disgusting monstrosity are ya?"

## Chapter Four

After a half hour of Hattie regaling them with more vacationer stories, the shop started to fill with some tourists on their way out of town. Gabe had to leave his post at Hattie's side to help Bill behind the counter.

For the next hour, Gabe took orders and made specialty coffees while Bill tried to entice people into his inedible breakfast sandwiches. Thankfully, no one took the bait.

This was the part of day Gabe loved and hated. The time went quickly because the shop was busy, but he had to deal with cranky tourists. By Monday, the mood of the travelers would change—because those folks would just be starting out their week here. But by Saturday morning, when folks were headed home, back to their dreary, non-beach lives, they grew a little testier. Gabe wondered why they came if their peace and relaxation didn't even last for the long ride home.

Coffee helped some folks be a little cheerier, but most took their orders with a scowl and moved on.

When the place had finally cleared a bit of the normal buzz of early morning chatter, Hattie declared she had to get home for her morning constitutional and shuffled out the door.

"Well, she was in a pretty rare mood today," Bill said, rinsing her mug and putting it with the others to be washed. "Wish she was that delightful every day."

Gabe grabbed a washrag and began filling the sink with hot water. "Her stories about tourists next to her house makes me glad I'm living here and not some place closer to the beach. I prefer to be away from those kinds of people."

"But her house is right on the beach, and you miss that perk too."

Gabe shrugged. "I can do without that. Besides I can go to the beach anytime anyway. It's just across the road and down the path. I can hear the surf from the back deck."

Bill took the first mug Gabe washed and began to dry it with a towel. Gabe could tell by the pregnant pause that his friend had more to say and waited for the other shoe to drop.

"When's the last time you spent any time on the beach?"

Gabe washed another mug from the day before and tried to think of a response.

At the age of forty-nine, Gabe had lived a pretty frugal life and had no debts. The sale of his house in Pennsylvania had left him with enough money for the move, some basic supplies, and a bit put into other savings he'd socked away for himself and Ellie. For their retirement. Which they now would never enjoy. At least not together.

But he'd given up a six-figure job to fulfill Ellie's dream of living near the beach and didn't want to simply waste money. His people were known to live long, *long* lives, so he'd need to keep up his frugal ways.

"I get to the beach now and again." It certainly wasn't a lie, but not wholly the truth either. He had spent a few days on the beach, but it hadn't felt right enjoying himself without Ellie. The look on Bill's face told him he wasn't fooling anyone.

"Come to the crab boil tonight. We're going to have a few other church friends over and we can watch the sunset."

The coffee shop and apartment were situated in the interior of the island, but Bill and his wife lived on the bay side. Gabe had never been to their house but knew the sunsets on the bay side were spectacular. Ellie had lived for sunrises and sunsets, especially while at the beach. She'd dragged him to many, kept him out late to watch them, even dealt with scads of tourists just to watch the pinks, blues, and reds paint the sky. A few years ago, they had rented a place right here in Avon with a hammock outside the master bedroom. Ellie had risen early every morning to lie in that hammock to watch the sun rise and then stayed out there every night after the sun went down to watch the stars.

*You should go, babe. The sunset will be worth it.*

"I'll think about it, but don't hold me to it. I still have my shift at the Food Lion too. I work until seven."

Bill sighed. "Fine, although I don't know why you work two jobs. But I think some of the other folks work until six anyway and won't be able to make it until after that. Come when you're done. I'll be sure to save you some." His boss winked. "Besides, you're probably hungry since you threw out half my bacon sandwich."

## Chapter Five

"Hey, you better get to stepping." Bill snapped Gabe lightly with a towel he'd been using to clean off a table four young tourists had mucked up. "It's almost two. Daisy needs to go out before you hit that other job, you know."

Gabe rearranged sugar packets for what felt like the tenth time today. "Those kids were drunk, you know that, right? I bet they hit one of those breweries up in Kill Devil Hills and then needed some coffee to sober up." Despite his righteous indignation, it was really jealousy Gabe felt. He wished he could lounge around all morning or afternoon or whole day in a brewery.

*You can. What's stopping you?*

He shoved the last sugar packet into the holder as he pushed away Ellie's voice in his head.

Bill walked into the kitchen with his stained towel and two dirty mugs. "Yeah. Drunk kids come in every once in a while. Glad there's only one road in and out of here, and most people take it at a moderate pace."

"Can't you see these idiots in their fancy sports cars stuck alongside the road in the sand, though?" The thought made Gabe smile, even though he'd once been one of those idiots. But a lot had changed since those younger years in his life.

Bill shrugged. "Gotta pray God will protect them, I guess."

Gabe sneered. "Some people are beyond prayer."

"I know you don't truly believe that." His coworker gave him a sideward glance as he plunged a mug into the hot, soapy water.

"I better get up there," Gabe said, sidestepping yet another conversation on religion. "Daisy will be crossing her legs right about now." Gabe whipped off his apron and strode to the back stairs, taking two at a time.

He hated being so abrupt but didn't feel like talking about God today—one of Bill's favorite topics. Bill and Gladys were very faithful to the Cape Hatteras Baptist Church and had even held Wednesday evening Bible studies in their home. They had invited Gabe to church every Sunday since he'd moved here, and he'd not gone once. Bill told him they frequently prayed for him, which he found only slightly comforting. Since Ellie had died, he hadn't felt much like talking to God.

He was still a Christian—God definitely sent his Son to die for his many sins—but his relationship with his heavenly Father was not what it once was. He found it hard to be friends with a guy who had taken away the love of his life way too soon. He still read the Bible on his phone occasionally, but he wasn't ready for the fake atmosphere most churches exuded. He recalled the children's Sunday school song he'd learned as a child about being happy all the time. Ugh! Why did they teach children that stuff? No wonder so many preachers' kids were messed up.

*Our church was wonderful, and you know it. Why did you leave?*

Daisy ran for her favorite purple rhino squeaky toy as he entered the apartment. She came bolting back to him with it in her mouth, butt wagging.

"Do you have any other speed?" he bent down to ask her, petting her head. She promptly dropped the rhino and gave him three fast slurps across his nose.

"Ugh!" He stood back up and wiped off his face. "Yes, kisses. While you're all wound up, we might as well take a quick walk."

Daisy lunged for the door, nearly knocking him over as he reached for the leash. After two attempts at snagging her, he finally heard the clasp catch, and they were out the door.

They traversed the same path they had walked this morning—down past several other shops on a cement walkway next to the busy highway. The road was much busier now than it had been early this morning.

A Jeep convertible sped by, occupants calling out greetings, waving, hooting, and hollering.

Gabe kept his focus on the sidewalk.

When they had made their little circle, and Daisy had squatted about fifteen times, Gabe directed the dog back to their little apartment. Once inside, he unclipped her leash, and Daisy dashed for the rhino once more. She ran over to his favorite chair and looked back at him forlornly.

"Sorry, girl, I got to get to the other job."

He'd taken on the other job at the local grocery store just to keep busy. When he'd moved here after Ellie's death, he'd needed to stay focused on something—to try and avoid her persistent voice in his head. He'd thought two jobs would keep him busy enough to handle his grief.

He'd been wrong.

He changed quickly into a black pair of slacks and a white polo then bolted out the door. Leaving his truck parked under the carport, he walked the half mile to the store. One thing that had improved since he'd moved here was his leg strength. If only he could lay off the beer at night and eat a few more veggies, he'd probably lose his gut too.

Arriving at the store as a trail of sweat trickled down his back, he clocked in and grabbed his green apron.

"Gabe! I didn't even realize it was three already."

His manager, Brent, stood by the loading dock, marking off inventory on a clipboard. The man rubbed Gabe the wrong way, but he wasn't sure why. Maybe it was the sheer fact he was in a position of authority over Gabe. Or maybe he reminded Gabe of the boss from his teenage years in Iowa's largest grocery store chain. Brent never gave Gabe any grief, but he was single and had often tried to get Gabe into the "club scene" around town.

"Hey, man, meet any new single ladies this morning at the coffeeshop?" Brent leered at him over his clipboard, then wriggled his eyebrows up and down. "Skimpy bikinis and all that?"

*Ugh. Yep, he's a sleaze.*

"Nope. Not a one."

"Bummer." Brent looked back at his clipboard. "I'm going to put you on produce today. You seem well suited to that."

Gabe nodded. He'd worked produce as a teenager too and loved it, except for the rotten fruits and veggies you sometimes put your finger right through. He remembered how Ellie had tried to get him to eat yams every Thanksgiving, but he'd refused. You can't eat those things once you have stuck your thumb through a rotten one.

He shook off a shudder and said, "Sounds good."

Brent pointed to a stack of boxes. "These can go out once you comb through everything for expired stuff. And remember, it's Saturday. It's madness out there and will only get worse as more folks get into town." His look turned lecherous again. "But maybe some hotties will come in today. I already spoke to one young thing who came in earlier." He fanned himself with the clipboard. "Whew! She was all that and a bag of chips, if you get my meaning."

*Where is he getting that reference? 1994?*

Gabe nodded again and pulled on a set of rubber gloves—a modern improvement to when he'd been a kid doing this job. At least he could pull off the glove now and not smell like rotten fruit for the rest of the day. And maybe if he got out onto the floor, he could shake off Brent and his ridiculous banter. Gabe did not want some "hot, young thing." He only wanted Ellie back. The thought of going on a date again, starting over, made him shudder.

He'd always told Ellie he'd never date again.

"Start all over? No thank you."

She had agreed. "I have you trained. You know how long that took me to get right? I could never start over."

They had laughed, thinking they'd never need to even think seriously about this idea since they were both young and in good health.

"Yeah, man, I tried to get her number, but she acted all hard to get, ya know?" Brent continued babbling on. "But I think she'll be back."

*For groceries maybe.*

After grabbing an empty box for the discards, Gabe pushed through the swinging doors and into the chaos.

"We'll catch up later!" Brent called after him.

*Not if I can help it.*

Families looking already beat down and worn out walked through the produce aisle like zombies. Some looked like they really needed a vacation. Good thing they were on one. The store was a small one but the sole grocery in town. The only other Food Lion was up in Nags Head, almost an hour away. Farther south were some smaller food stores, but the Food Lion had the best selection. At least until the hordes came through every Saturday and Sunday. Then the staff here scrambled to keep shelves stocked.

He remembered the days of traveling to the outer banks, or OBX as it was locally called, with his family and then his wife and friends. That first shopping trip was always the worst as you tried to get in and get out but not knowing exactly what you would need for the week. Or needing to think on the fly when they didn't have what you wanted. And the produce aisle was never great in the small grocery store. Even though the supply truck came several times a day, the produce was never very stellar to begin with. That's why those farm markets on the mainland did such good business every year—the produce was much better there. He'd liked to think he'd improved the selection here some, but the store could still only put out what they had.

He worked through the bagged lettuces first, once nearly losing his hand to a young lady with four kids surrounding her.

"Ma'am, I think that's a little overripe," he said, trying to take the bag from her. "Let me get you a better bag." He'd pulled down a fresher one and handed it to her, but she'd grabbed the new bag with a scowl and tossed the other bag at Gabe. It fell to the floor, and he sighed.

*Tourists. Next time, I'll just let her have the spoiled stuff.*

By six thirty, he'd combed through every square inch of the produce aisle, unloaded a supply truck, and added fresh product in place of the rotten stuff he'd discarded. The crowds had not thinned once but had only grown larger. Despite his best efforts, large gaps still showed in the aisle, and another truck was not due until tomorrow. As he attempted to rearrange the bell peppers to fill the area, Brent came up and slapped him on the back.

"I hear Bill and Gladys are having a crab boil tonight. You going?"

"Maybe." Gabe kept his focus on the produce, secretly wishing his boss would walk away and let him do his thing.

"I invited this hottie I saw earlier. She said she'd meet me there."

Gabe wondered what the odds of that truly happening were.

"I'm heading out now, in fact." Brent stood back from Gabe and looked around. "You did a good job today. Can't help it we can't keep up with the demand." He stepped up then and removed the bell peppers from Gabe's hands. "This girl said she had a friend, and I told her to bring her along. Wanted to make sure you had someone to talk to." He waggled his eyebrows in that leering way again, and Gabe fought back the urge to puke. "You've put in a good day's work. Clock out and head to Bill's." He threw the peppers into an empty slot, and Gabe grimaced.

"I would really like to finish." He eyed the peppers and scanned the remaining empty bins.

"You know these folks don't care what it looks like, right? They want to get out to their decks with a beer and enjoy their vacation. No one eats vegetables on vacation anyway."

The empty slots throughout the produce aisle indicated otherwise, but Gabe still said, "I like to finish what I start."

Brent patted him again on the shoulder. "I hope you don't miss your chance with this girl. I might take both for myself if you don't show." He sneered again but then scowled when Gabe didn't give him the response he wanted. "Fine, but clock out before seven, or I'll hear it from brass."

Brent walked away, sidestepping several families who were contemplating the value of the deep green bananas Gabe had put out earlier.

He breathed a sigh of relief. To be left alone was his greatest goal. He'd taken this job thinking he'd have a lot of solitude. Normally, he didn't like alone time anymore, but this empty time space included work that kept his mind busy without needing to chat with anyone—like at the coffee shop. The job filled that need—except for Brent's constant urging to hook up with some tourist. He'd never been someone to "hook up" anyway. And he hated that term. What did it even mean? Like a fish caught on a hook?

Turning back to the display, he picked up the discarded peppers Brent had thrown—did the man not know anything about produce? Rearranging them neatly next to the others, he turned to survey his work. For the most part, the aisle looked good, even though he knew his hard work would be destroyed within the hour as the last few tourists descended into town. Tomorrow would probably be just as bad. He straightened a few more areas in the produce section, then helped a short old man snag some radishes from the top bin. The man walked away without even a simple thank you.

Sighing, Gabe walked to the back room, pulling at the strings of his apron as he went. After he'd clocked out, he contemplated stopping at Bill's for a quick hello and even quicker goodbye. He could feign tiredness. He'd worked two jobs today, after all. Then he thought of Brent and the potential for two tourist women looking for a good time, and he reconsidered. He'd get sucked in for longer than he wanted or trapped by overzealous horndog Brent. Worse yet, ensnared by Bill and his Bible verses. Gabe made his way back to his apartment instead.

## Chapter Six

After feeding Daisy, Gabe plopped down on his recliner with a cold bottle of beer in one hand and his laptop in the other. Daisy nudged his arm, hoping to share some space with him on the chair. He cringed as a splash of beer landed on his armchair.

"Go lay down."

The hound hung her head and gave him the best forlorn look she could muster before turning and moping to her bed. She flopped down much as he'd done in his own chair and heaved a huge sigh.

"Yep, I know. I'm the worst."

He took a swig from the cold bottle, opened his laptop and then his email program.

Another email from his sister, urging him to reply and asking when she could visit.

A long rambling message from his friend in Iowa, complaining about his life—a normal occurrence.

And several spam items attempting to entice him to immoral activities or to sell him something he didn't need.

He deleted them all without replying and turned to the folder marked "Us."

## Sue A. Fairchild

Gabe,
It was so great to be with you this past weekend. I cried and cried when you left, though. I know that might sound crazy since we've only known each other a short while, but I feel such a connection to you. The physical distance between us drives me crazy. I wonder what God's plan is for us if we're so far apart. Do you think this will work? Maybe you don't feel the same way and I'm being silly. But I'm growing so fond of you already and it's scary, but I want to see where it goes. I hope you do too.
Talk soon, Ellie

One of her first emails to him. He'd felt the same way and had told her so in a reply email. They had only been seeing each other for about a month. But both knew God had something in store when they had met.

He'd been much closer to God in those days. He'd worked audio for his church and had spent more time there than at home—Wednesday nights and almost all day Sunday. He'd been active with the church family too, attending BBQs and social nights, participating in the cantatas and some of the small groups. He used to do Bible reading every morning before work and kept a journal of what he learned.

Now he couldn't even remember where his Bible was. Although he and Ellie had also been active in their church, when she'd died, he'd stepped away from all activities. His cousin who attended the same church had tried to engage him time and again, but he'd shut her out. He wondered how her kids were doing now. He'd not spoken to her since moving here.

He felt a prickle of regret but quickly washed it down with a swig of his beer.

*You always put up walls.*

Yep. He sure did. And he liked it inside his little private sanctuary. No one to hurt him. No one to deal with except himself.

Daisy whined from her spot, and he scowled in her direction.

"Except for you." He frowned and took another swig of his beer.

He wondered now if God still had a plan for his life. He'd seen the plan so clearly back then—marry Ellie, make her happy, be happy. But what was the plan now? Surely it was not to just work until he died, was it?

They had been introduced by a mutual friend, but he'd lived over five hundred miles away at the time. Their email correspondence was the only thing they had going for them at the beginning. He clicked on his response email.

> Ellie,
> Yes, I feel the same. There is something here for sure, and I want us to explore it. Who knows, maybe God will move one of us soon, and we'll get married and … No, scratch that. Too fast.
> I look forward to seeing you again. Can you come here next time? If not, I'll rearrange my schedule to get to you.
> Gabe

He laughed, then took another swig of beer. He'd been smitten so quickly but didn't want to play his cards. Yet, he'd trusted God then and knew with almost certainty they would marry. Three years later, after God moved him closer to her with a new job and the advantageous sale of his townhouse, they did. He'd told Ellie he knew after their first date that he'd marry her.

Gabe scrolled through hundreds of emails, talking about mundane things, moving plans, wedding plans … they had talked about everything and emailed each other up to five times a day sometimes. His email folder topped over ten thousand emails. He'd recently taken the extra step of saving some of the most important ones to an offline file.

When they started dating, they had come up with "deal breakers" that neither could live with. He found the email that outlined hers. Although they had talked about it in an epic five-hour phone call, she'd felt the need to have it in writing. Ellie put everything in writing. Her list had been simple: non-smoker, non-abusive, faithful to her and God. His had been simple too—yet complicated—no kids. She'd taken some time to contemplate that one, and he'd feared he was going to lose her. But, in the end, she'd agreed.

Now he felt as if his demand was just another thing he'd failed at giving her—another happiness he'd prevented. She mentioned to him once or twice she was unsure they had made the right decision. He often wondered if she regretted not having kids or perhaps felt bitter toward him about it. She said not—especially after they had spent time with his cousins' kids—but he still wondered.

When he'd read all he cared to of the emails, he turned to the text thread he'd kept on his phone. He scrolled back through the last few texts Ellie had sent. They didn't text much, preferring to email instead. But one caught his eye.

**Are you coming right home tonight?**

Gabe hadn't known why she was asking and had told her he thought so. But the boss had come in just as he was getting ready to leave. When he'd finally made it home an hour late, he'd found Ellie on the floor sobbing with Daisy licking her face. He ran to her, and she'd told him about the call she'd gotten from the doctor about a recent scan. She'd been having pain in her abdomen for months, so the doctor had ordered some tests, but neither he nor Ellie had thought much of it. She'd had gastrointestinal issues for years. But the diagnosis that day would change their lives forever and would rip the life away from his soulmate.

Gabe took a deep breath and clicked to read her text over and over again.

**Are you coming right home tonight?**

Why hadn't he told the boss he was heading home instead of acquiescing to her last-minute request for a "quick" meeting? Now he grieved over every lost second he hadn't spent with Ellie. He'd wanted to take more time off at the end too, but she'd told him no. Ellie always put up a strong front no matter what she was feeling. Something her dad had taught her. Something they both had in common.

"Dad showed me the only one who can get things done is me. Don't rely on others. Just get it done. Don't let anything get in your way."

Even a cancer diagnosis, it seemed.

Her strength was one of the things he loved about her—she could be strong, but she'd also needed him when she couldn't. Yet, he should have spent more time with her. Gone to more appointments with her. Listened to her voice, touched her face, held her tightly. Ellie had made several videos for her business that she'd posted on YouTube, and he went there often just to hear her voice. But to hold her in his arms again ... oh, what he wouldn't give.

He got up to grab another bottle of beer from the fridge and threw the empty into the recycling bin. Daisy followed him through the living room and into the kitchen and back again, but he ignored her attempts at affection. He didn't have any to give anymore.

As he sat back down and drank some beer from his bottle, Gabe thought about the months following her diagnosis. At first, Ellie had refused treatment.

"This is God's will for me. I told you before I couldn't fight something like this."

But Gabe had argued, cajoled, pleaded with her, and she'd relented once again. She'd often given in to his way, and now he felt dirty because of it.

She'd suffered months of radiation and chemo treatments. He could still feel the helplessness as he stood outside their bathroom door while she retched out the poison in her system. When she'd lost hair and weight, her already low self-esteem had taken a dramatic tumble.

Finally, she'd called enough and quit every treatment. He'd let her. Not because he'd given up too, but because he couldn't see her suffer anymore. Maybe it was God's will.

Gabe choked back a sob as he remembered how he'd railed at God all during that time. Calling him every nasty word in the book. Blaming him for everything.

Daisy raised her head from her bed with her ears laid back as if to say, "You all right, Papa?" He waved his beer bottle at her and drained it.

"Grief sucks, Daisy. Be glad you don't have feelings."

But he knew she did. Their pup had mourned Ellie almost as much as he had. Daisy had laid by their bed for a week after Ellie's funeral. She'd refused to eat. Only when Gabe had come out of his own stupor and fed her bacon and beef did she start to come around. She still sniffed Ellie's side of the bed on occasion and whined, even though he'd washed the sheets many times.

He rose to grab another beer and realized it had grown dark in the house, the glow from his laptop the only light. He snapped on a lamp and went to the kitchen. The near empty fridge stared back at him—only a small bit of cooked elbow noodles and sauce remained. His stomach grumbled. He couldn't remember when he'd eaten last today—*Oh right, the bacon sandwich from this morning*—but the thought of eating the noodles for the fifth night in a row was less than appetizing.

He should have picked up something after work at the grocery store or gone to the crab boil. But it was too late now. Closing the fridge door, he turned to rummage around in a cabinet. He found a stale pack of peanut butter crackers. *Protein. That will do for now.* He shoved one dry cracker into his mouth and wished for another beer. He reached into the cabinet for a glass and his hand bumped something off to the side. Pulling it out, he saw the half empty bottle of bourbon Ellie had purchased a few months before her death.

"If I'm already being poisoned, I might as well do it with something fun," she'd said.

Gabe hated liquor. Could never stand the stuff. He told Ellie it smelled and tasted like gasoline. Why had he packed this?

He stared at the bottle and tried to remember his thought process in packing the offending liquid. He'd not been in his right mind, he supposed. He thought of the few pieces of Ellie's clothes that hung now at the back of his closet and the boxes of other stuff—full of he wasn't sure what—in the corner of the bedroom. His sister had helped him get rid of some of Ellie's clothes, but he'd kept a few pieces that still smelled like Ellie or reminded him of her.

He grabbed a glass and poured a few fingers of the brown spirit into it. He stared at the liquor for another minute before returning to his chair with the glass and the remaining crackers.

After taking a large gulp of the stuff and forcing it down his gullet, he coughed for a full three minutes. *This must be what drinking fire feels like.* Now he remembered why he hated this stuff. Tomorrow, he'd stock up on more beer. But for tonight, the liquid was already starting to do its work as he felt his head grow fuzzy.

Before the stuff had a chance to really knock him out, he typed a quick email to his sister.

> Doing OK. Getting settled in still. Life here is different. I'm not really ready for company yet, tho. My place is super small. Maybe for the holidays, I'll come see you? I'll let you know.

The holidays.

Ellie had loved Thanksgiving and Christmas. They always had a big, juicy turkey for Thanksgiving, even after her parents had died and it had been just them. They had eaten turkey sandwiches, turkey divan, and turkey casserole for days after. Her stuffing had been the best too. He wondered briefly if he'd packed her recipe box and where it might be now. *Maybe in those boxes.*

And Christmas. Oh, she'd gone all out for Christmas. He'd hated the holiday because they had never really celebrated it when he was a kid, but she lived for it, demanding he help her decorate the tree and string up lights on the porch. He'd not done a thing last year, and he'd felt relieved of the chore.

Except part of him still wanted to.

Last year had been tough—those first holidays after Ellie's death were the hardest. After Ellie's parents had died, they'd spent the holidays with his sister and sometimes his parents who lived out west, but last year he'd refused. He'd wanted to pretend the holidays didn't exist. But what most people didn't understand is the loneliness one feels during the holidays if you didn't celebrate the day. Most stores are closed on Christmas, and the only place to eat is Chinese restaurants. The only thing on TV are sappy Christmas movies. When Gabe had taken Daisy for a walk on Christmas Day, hoping to do something normal to pass the time, the squeals of fun and joy coming from his neighbors' homes had hit him in the gut so hard he'd stood on the street and cried. He'd felt so alone. He'd eaten a large portion of General Tso's and rice, drunk a six pack of beer, and gone to bed at six.

He knew he'd kept some of her Christmas decorations, but not many. *Were they in those boxes too?*

He crumpled up the cracker package and walked to the kitchen to throw it out and grab a glass of water this time. Daisy picked up her head again, her eyes now bleary. His own were starting to go that way too, but he still needed to take Daisy out once more today.

"Okay, girl, Let's go out. One last time today and then off to bed."

The dog sprang up at the word "out" and was already prancing around his feet, stuffed toy—the squirrel one this time—shoved in her mouth. He swayed a bit, wondering how he'd make it down the stairs. After several attempts, he clipped on the leash, and they were out the door.

Gabe tugged on Daisy's leash and made her go slowly down the steps, each one looking like two and narrower than they actually were. He put one foot out in front and stepped forward, hoping he'd not misjudge. When he had made it to the ground, he heaved a sigh of relief.

"Okay, girl, just out and back. Don't think I can do much … much more." He let out a belch and smiled. Ellie hated when he was so uncouth. But now there was no one to care. His smile faded.

As they walked and Daisy sniffed, Gabe's head swam, and he thought back to that diagnosis, the months of treatment, and that last day when he'd gone out for … He swallowed hard and swiped at the tears forming in his eyes. He'd decided to move after those first disastrous holidays without her and her first birthday in heaven. He'd sold most of the life they had accumulated together and moved to the beach where she'd always wanted to live.

Daisy pulled at the leash, and he stopped, rummaging for the plastic bag he'd need. Even those reminded him of his dead wife, how they never used the resealable bags for anything other than Daisy's daily deposits.

Gabe and Daisy returned to the house, his fog already beginning to lift. He wished he had more beer but refused to drink anymore of the fire water. He locked the door and put Daisy's leash on its hook—just like he'd done in his old life. Beach living didn't seem much different to Gabe, and he wondered briefly if there was something he was missing. Maybe Bill was right—he needed to spend more time at the beach. Ellie sure would have. She longed to have the sun on her skin every day and feel its warmth. Gabe smiled as he remembered her constantly cold feet—even in summertime.

"If you ever retire," she'd said, "we're heading south. I need the sun!"

"Of course we'll move, Babe. I promise I'll give you everything you have ever wanted once I retire."

Gabe's heart ached as he remembered those words. If only he'd known she'd never live at the beach. If only he'd known how short a time they really had. Would he have done things differently? Would he have provided more things for her happiness?

As his head hit the pillow, he thought about all the things he'd never given Ellie and his heart ached.

## Chapter Seven

Gabe woke as he'd the day before, this time with a fiercer headache.

*Stupid bourbon.*

He stared at the ceiling and rubbed his temple with one finger. *Five days to go.*

Daisy whined at the door as she did every day, and he groaned. Gabe briefly considered going to Bill's church. There was still time before the service, but he'd have to hurry. As he sat up in bed, his head throbbed, and he quickly reconsidered.

*Maybe I'll go to church next week.*

Then he thought about the beach. Maybe he should give it a try. The salty sea air would clear his pounding head. Deciding today would be as good a day as any, he shuffled to the bathroom and slathered on some sunscreen. Once properly covered to prevent his light skin from frying, he moved to the kitchen, Daisy at his heels.

"Got to take care of something first, pup."

He reached for the bourbon bottle, uncorked it, and held it over the sink. But as he was about to pour, his heart lurched. He hated the stuff, but this had been Ellie's. Her last bit of normal as the chemo had ravaged her body. One of the few things she could still stomach—surprisingly. He choked back a sob and replaced the stopper. *Now I remember why I packed it.* He shoved the bottle back into the cupboard and turned to Daisy.

He quickly leashed her, and they were out the door.

One step outside into the already bright day made his head throb harder, and he returned to the apartment to grab a ballcap. One downside of wearing glasses meant no sunglasses to block the bright day.

Daisy pulled Gabe toward the sidewalk from the coffee shop out to the main highway through Avon. Cars zipped past now at greater intervals and he remembered—Sunday. The tourists' first day in town. Internally, he groaned, but then he pressed forward, crossing Route 12 with Daisy running to catch up. He hoped he was early enough to avoid most of the tourist beachgoers as he strode down a shell-lined road. Several large rental homes loomed next to the road and seemed to grow the closer he got to the beach. He wondered how many bedrooms some of them had—knowing some friends who often came with their entire family. Like twelve to twenty people sometimes. He shuddered. How could you spend a week with that many people?

As he neared the beach, he saw a familiar person shuffling his way. Hattie.

Dressed in neon green shorts and a sparkly green shirt today, she looked as if she'd been to a dance club the night before but had changed into shorts only for her walk. He shook his head at her fashion sense.

"Gabriel, how are you this fine morning?" she called as she neared. "Where you headed?"

"The beach."

She stopped moving forward and tapped her cane. "Really? Thought you didn't go to the beach."

"I go ... occasionally."

Daisy strained at the leash, and Gabe fought to keep her in check.

"Let her come. She won't hurt these strong bones."

"She sometimes jumps. I don't want her to knock you down."

Hattie waved a hand then plopped down on the sandy road on her own terms. "Now we got that settled. Come, pretty girl!"

Daisy lunged at the old woman, and Gabe briefly closed his eyes, praying this was not a lawsuit waiting to happen. When he opened his eyes, the hound had sat down neatly next to Hattie and was licking her face while the old woman laughed heartily.

"Aren't you just the sweetest! Oh my word. Yes, girl ..."

"Her name's Daisy."

"Daisy," Hattie cooed. "Aren't you the bee's knees? Yes, you are." She ran a hand over the pup's ears as Daisy stretched her neck for scratches. "Oh, you need that, huh? You got it, sister."

Gabe couldn't help the smile on his face, but then had to fight back another wave of grief as an image of Ellie saying the same things to Daisy hit him hard.

When Daisy had enough attention, she meandered away to sniff the tall grasses beside the road. Hattie used her sparkly cane and struggled to stand. Gabe rushed to her and held out a hand for support.

"Thanks, dear. Getting down is the easy part. Gettin' up, I'm slower than molasses in winter." She smiled at him as she brushed sand off her backside and then gestured to Daisy. "You two can come use my pool any time, you know. Just give me a heads up and"—She gave him a wink—"no skinny dipping."

Gabe laughed outright and said, "Thanks for the offer. I'll give it some thought."

Hattie squinted at him in the fast-rising sun. "What do you do for fun, Gabriel? I know you're not just holing up in that apartment. Bill told me your story." When Gabe didn't respond, she continued. "Lost my love too, ya know. Going on five years now. My Harold. Such a louse sometimes, but I loved the old coot. Gave me all I ever wanted and by that, I mean a nice retirement plan and time left with him to spend it." She stopped and put a hand on Gabe's elbow. "Sorry. I shouldn't have said that. My durn mouth just does what it wants these days."

He waved her off. "I'm sorry for your loss. He sounds like a great guy."

"Eh." She tapped her cane again. "He was all right. Ran around on me a time or two, but he always came back." She leaned in close and whispered, "'Cuz he knew who buttered his biscuits." She cackled and slapped Gabe's arm, making Daisy run back and bounce at her side.

"Daisy, down!" Gabe grabbed the leash, and the pup sat, panting.

"Well, dear, I better git to going. If I don't get my walk in every day, these old bones just don't keep moving as they should."

"My wife used to say the same thing—" Gabe shut his mouth as he realized what he'd said. He'd never mentioned Ellie to anyone here except Bill, and that was only after the jerk had pried it from him.

Hattie leaned in again and gave his wrist a squeeze. "Ain't gonna hurt none to talk about her, Gabriel. Might actually help. I'm guessing she was a large part of your life."

When Gabe remained silent, she nodded her head and turned to walk away. "My offer still stands for the pool. I've got beer and liquor and sweet tea too. We can sit and chat about grief ... or not." She smiled and waved as she strode away, moving faster than Gabe thought possible for the older woman.

## Chapter Eight

As Gabe and Daisy crested the dune, he realized they had spent too much time chatting with Hattie. The beachfront was already crawling with tourists—kids with boogie boards, kids building sandcastles, and others of all ages lounging in the sun. Daisy pulled forward, though, longing to get into the surf. He'd only brought her out here one other time, and although she'd been fearful at first, she'd soon jumped and splashed in the waves. Now she pulled him forward, and he let the leash go slack so she could jump into the sea.

They found an empty spot near the edge of the water, and Daisy nipped and barked at the waves as they pushed up onto the shore. A calm ocean day, Gabe noticed. He wondered if he would experience his first hurricane this season. All sorts of tales already circulated about people waiting them out or having to evacuate. He'd nowhere to go, so he wasn't sure what he would do. Perhaps he would have to seek shelter all the way back in Virginia with his sister.

"Your dog is gorgeous."

Gabe turned at the compliment and took a sharp breath. A woman, looking very much like his dead wife, stood a few paces to his left. She wore a black, one-piece bathing suit with a white sarong covering her bottom half. Ellie had worn a similar outfit at the beach. The woman's hair was pulled up in a sloppy ponytail, but he could see wisps of curls falling out. He thought of Ellie's unruly mane of curls and how she fought to keep it up in buns or ponytails. The humidity of the beach always made the task extra difficult.

"Um." The woman took a step closer. "I said your dog is very pretty."

Gabe realized he hadn't replied and quickly recovered. He plastered on a fake smile and said, "Thanks. She's my wife's dog." *Now why did I say that?* "I mean, she *was* her dog." He felt his face flush. Had he grown so unaccustomed to small talk?

The woman's smile faltered for a brief second before saying, "Can I photograph her?" She held up a professional-looking camera and raised her eyebrows.

Gabe nodded. She put the camera to her eye and began snapping pics.

"She really loves the waves," she said, looking over the top of the viewfinder.

Just then, Daisy noticed the lady and came bounding from the ocean, water spraying both of them. The woman laughed as she bent down to greet the pup.

"Oh my! Yes, the water is lovely, isn't it, sweetie?"

"Her name's Daisy," Gabe supplied as he watched his traitorous dog lick the woman's face. He noticed this woman was thinner than Ellie had been—obviously not someone who struggled with weight issues the way his wife had. Ellie certainly would have walked up to someone to photograph or pet their dog, though. A wave of emotion choked his throat, and he looked away—out to the horizon to gather his wits.

When he looked back, Daisy had returned to the seaside, and the woman had stepped closer to him but was once again snapping pictures.

Finally, she lowered the camera and smiled at him. "Thanks. I needed my dog fix. She's quite wonderful. Mine passed away about six months ago." The woman put her hand to her brow to block the sun as she watched Daisy frolic.

"Oh, I'm sorry. My wife passed away about a year ago."

He longed to be one of the many tiny sand crabs burrowing into holes in that moment.

She turned to him with a furrowed brow, and he realized again how foolish he sounded. This woman didn't need his grief history. She simply had wanted to pet his dog. He twisted the leash in his hands.

"I'm so sorry," she whispered, so low he barely heard her above the crashing waves.

He looked back to his dog who was now jumping around the beach, chasing those lucky sand crabs.

The silence between them lengthened, and Gabe wished she would walk away and let him get on with his solitary life. She cleared her throat and said, "Where are you from?"

"Here. I just moved here six months ago."

"Oh, that must be such a great lif—" Her words cut off abruptly, and she mumbled, "Sorry."

"It was my wife's dream to live at the beach. I moved here to make her happy." Gabe continued to twist the leash in his hands. "I was a little late."

She offered him a sad smile and turned back to the sea. "Sometimes we don't see what's important until it's too late." She put the camera to her face again and took a few photos of the ocean stretching out before them. She looked at the pics she'd taken on the screen, deleted one, and turned to him once more.

He certainly agreed with her assessment. But enough about him. If she wanted conversation, he didn't want it to be about him. "Where are you from? I don't think you're a local."

"No." She shook her head and laughed. "I'm out here ... just taking some time away." She stuck out her hand. "I'm Nora."

"Gabe," he said and shook her hand.

"I'm in a place back off the beach a bit." She pointed directly behind them. "My first time here. It's lovely."

Gabe nodded and turned back to see Daisy digging with abandon. "Hey!" he called. "Stop that!" He tugged on the leash and Daisy looked up for a moment before returning to her task. He sighed as he heard Nora snapping a few more pics of his rebellious pup.

"I've got to get her home and cleaned up. Enjoy your stay."

"Thanks. Maybe we'll run into each other again."

Gabe gave the idea some thought but pushed it away as he dragged Daisy from her now significant hole. "Maybe," he called to Nora and waved over his shoulder.

When he and Daisy had crested the top of the dune, he looked back but couldn't see Nora, who was now mixed in the crowd of people lounging on the beach. *Why is it this crowded? It's the end of the season.* He thought he spotted her for a moment, but the woman turned, and he realized she was older and her suit a dark shade of navy, not black. And he didn't see the camera.

Some new beach goers came over the dune, and he scooted out of the way, holding Daisy back. Then he trudged down the dune and back toward home.

## Chapter Nine

Later that day, Gabe was considering taking a quick trip to the store for some supplies when a knock came at his door. After commanding Daisy to sit, he turned and opened the door.

Bill stood with an armload full of supplies and a six pack of beer. Daisy, sensing her friend, nudged Gabe away and jumped at Bill's overloaded arms.

Bill smiled but stepped back. "Hey, girl! Get down." To Gabe he said, "Better let me in before the hound rips me to shreds."

Gabe opened the door wide, and Bill ushered Daisy and himself in. He put the packages and the beer on the counter that separated the living room and kitchen. Once empty handed, he bent down on one knee to lavish attention on Daisy. She promptly rolled over onto her back to demand belly scratches.

"Ha. You're something else, dog. I know Gabe here doesn't give you any sort of attention."

"I took her to the beach this morning so she could play in the surf. I think she's got it pretty good."

Bill looked up with raised eyebrows. "You went to the beach?"

"Yeah, and what a mistake. Tourists everywhere. Isn't this the off season?"

Bill stood, leaving Daisy on her back. "Not technically. But soon. Still there does seem to be a lot more folks this time." He turned to the bags and began unpacking. "Come here and help, since this is for you anyway."

Gabe strode into the kitchen and began putting items away as Bill handed them to him. Leftovers from the crab boil. A few slices of pie. A container of milk.

"You didn't have to do this, you know. I was just about to go out and get stuff."

Bill came into the kitchen holding a loaf of bread and peered into the nearly empty fridge. "Yeah, sure looks like you have been keeping yourself well stocked." He smirked.

"I have the essentials." He pointed to the almost empty milk jug and a container of salsa.

"Seriously? What is that?" Bill motioned to another container within the sparse fridge.

"Cooked elbow noodles." How had he missed that the other night?

"You eat those plain or what?" Bill grabbed the six pack. "Care to share this with me?"

Gabe nodded as Bill took two from the pack and put the rest in the fridge. "I eat the noodles with the salsa."

Bill shuddered visibly, and Gabe pushed him out of the kitchen. "We can sit out on the deck if you want."

"You have chairs out there?"

"We could drag out kitchen chairs." Gabe had not brought much with him and most things he didn't readily need—like beach chairs—had been left packed in his truck.

"Let's sit on the couch. More comfortable anyway," Bill suggested.

The two men walked to the living room where Daisy had taken up her stuffed toy, looking forlorn.

"You don't need pets every second," Gabe told her. She dropped her rhino and plunked her chin down on top of it, eyes in their standard sad puppy dog look.

"She really lays it on thick, doesn't she?" Bill asked as he parked himself on the couch.

"Yes, she had Ellie wrapped around her finger with those looks, but I'm a cold-hearted jerk."

Bill harrumphed and took a swig of his beer. He looked around the apartment. "You didn't do much with the place. Don't you have anything to hang on the walls?"

Gabe took a pull of his beer and shrugged. "Isn't important to me, I guess. I've got some pics in the bedroom."

He looked around the space now and realized how bland the whole place looked. Ellie had been the decorator, putting her art degree to use to make their space look lived in and welcoming. The apartment had come with basic blinds on all the windows, and that's about it. Gabe had moved in his well-worn recliner, his couch, a coffee table that Ellie's dad had made years ago, and a small folding table to go by the recliner. But he'd not hung a thing on the walls in the main living space. In the bedroom, he'd hung several photos of himself and Ellie, including one larger wedding photo. He knew he had some other things packed away in boxes. Maybe it was time to get those out and see what else he had brought along. He'd been in a fog when he'd packed up their things—putting some things into boxes to donate while packing up others to bring with him. He wasn't even sure what he had.

"Kind of looks like a college dorm in here, man. Maybe get a plant or something to liven up the place."

"Naw, I got a black thumb. It wouldn't last long anyway so why put it through that?" Gabe rose from the couch and grabbed the bag of little cheese pretzels Bill had brought. "Sorry I don't have a bowl. We'll have to eat out of the bag."

"Doesn't bother me none. Gladys likes to do that—put everything into fancy bowls. Seems like a waste to me 'cuz you're just going to have to wash that bowl later."

Gabe nodded his agreement and fisted a handful of pretzels into his mouth as he sat back down on the couch. He'd not had this kind since before … He nearly choked on a crumb and began coughing. Bill smacked his back a few times before handing him his beer. Gabe took a swig and swallowed hard.

"Sorry, down the wrong pipe."

"I would have left them out if I knew they were going to kill you."

Gabe chuckled and shook his head. "No, I'm a dumb eater. I always breathe in when I'm trying to chew, and particles go into my throat. Used to scare the crap out of Ellie all the time."

"Well, she cared about you."

Gabe turned away from Bill's sympathetic look. He didn't need anyone's pity. He was strong. He was doing fine. He shoved more pretzels in his mouth.

After chewing for a bit and, thankfully, not coughing again, he said, "Anyway, did you just come by to ensure I'm still alive and to provide further sustenance?"

"Gladys suggested it since you didn't stop by for the crab boil last night. Brent stopped by and seemed surprised you weren't there. Said he'd set up some hot dates for the two of you." Bill rolled his eyes.

"And I didn't want any hot date. Did those girls even come?"

Bill nodded. "Two really young girls did show up, but then saw how lame our old people party was and split."

He laughed. "Brent tried to follow them until I pointed out their obvious age differences. He sulked around the back yard for a bit before heading home." Bill eyed Gabe over his bottle. "So you didn't come just because you didn't want to be set up?"

Gabe took another pull of his beer as he tried to think of a good excuse. "I didn't feel like being social." The truth wasn't always such a bad thing. "With anyone."

"Yeah, I get it. Gladys had me running back and forth from the kitchen and patio. I think I lost five pounds from all the running. But, man, you missed a good meal." He gestured to the kitchen. "Gladys packed up some stuff, but it's not the same as fresh."

"Tell her thanks for me."

"You can tell her yourself if you come to dinner some night this week. She thinks you're living the bachelor life over here." He looked around and said, "Which it seems you are."

Gabe rose to grab another beer without answering him. He pulled out two and motioned to Bill.

"Naw, I better get back before she sends out the hounds. No offense, Daisy."

The pup stood and stretched at the sound of her name and then padded over to Bill. When he reached to pat her head, she promptly swung around and presented her butt instead.

"She prefers butt scratches," Gabe told him.

Bill laughed and dug his nails into the dog's backside. "Ask and ye shall receive." Daisy raised her nose and moved her butt back and forth with delight at Bill's expert scratching. When he stopped, she looked back at him again with those forlorn eyes, but he said, "I got to run, pup." To Gabe he said, "You should bring her into the shop tomorrow. People will love it, and she'll have more people to adore her."

"I'll think about it. I don't want her getting in the way."

"We'll put some blankets down for her—or bring her bed—so she has somewhere to go if she gets tired. The tourists will love her. And you'll love it too, won't you, girl?" He gave her butt one more scratch and stood. "And you better get yourself some more groceries, mister. That stuff I brought won't last long."

"I don't eat much these days," Gabe said as he drained his beer bottle.

"You better lay off that stuff then if there's nothing else in your stomach."

Gabe shrugged and walked Bill to the door. "I said I was just about to go out."

Bill patted him on the shoulder. "It'll get better, my friend. I promise."

Gabe shrugged off his hand. "I'm not sure I believe that."

Bill leaned up against the door jamb and said, "When I lost my first wife—"

"Wait. Gladys isn't your first wife?"

"Nope. Phyllis Jean Martin was my first wife. The first girl I ever dated, in fact. Swept me right off my feet."

"How did she die?" Gabe realized his faux pas the minute the words had left his mouth. "Sorry. I hate when people ask me. I have my mother's penchant for saying the first thing that comes to my head."

Bill paused for a moment, and Gabe saw something move through his eyes—a wave of grief, he supposed, much like he'd been feeling. "Car accident."

"How long ago was that?" Gabe couldn't help himself. He knew he hated these same questions, but he'd not talked to anyone else about their grief, and he suddenly felt a sort of kinship with his new friend.

Bill stood up straight then and cleared his throat. "Twenty years ago."

*Twenty years* ... "So, it doesn't ever get better then, does it?" Gabe crossed his arms over his chest.

"It does. But I can't tell you the pain goes away completely. I still miss her sometimes ... well, no, all the time, but sometimes it's not as heavy as it used to be. Gladys helps. My work helps. Doing things for my church and community helps." Bill poked a finger into Gabe's chest. "But I can tell you what didn't help. Sitting around feeling sorry for myself. That only works for a time. You have to get on with the business of life, my friend."

Gabe took a step away from Bill's finger and said, "I'm getting on with life."

Bill shook his head as he moved through the door. "No. You're getting on with *her* life. You got to get on with *yours*."

## Chapter Ten

The next morning, Gabe woke early, Bill's statement still ringing in his mind. Could what he said be true? Is that why he'd not been able to work through his grief yet, because he was just trying to live the life Ellie had envisioned instead of the one he wanted for himself?

They had both talked about moving south in retirement—he'd wanted it too. But he'd always thought he'd work at his corporate job until he was at least sixty-five. Ellie had always lamented how being older than him meant she would probably never see the warm south as a home. He'd assured her they would make that dream a reality, but cancer had ruined those plans.

As he walked Daisy and readied himself for work, regret and guilt reared their ugly heads. Why had he waited? They could have found jobs at the beach or inland, and Ellie wouldn't have suffered through every northern winter. Her moods often shifted in the winter, and she complained of cold feet and hands no matter how high they turned the thermostat or the layers of clothes she wore.

He'd seen it all as a minor inconvenience, just something they had to wait on. But now he wondered how he could have kept her from her dream.

He wanted to give it all back to her now. He wanted to give her everything she desired. But now he could only live the life she had dreamed of in honor of her. He knew it was not enough.

He trudged down the back stairs and into the coffee shop as Bill was unlocking the front door and turning the open sign.

"Hey! You're up early today," Bill said as a customer walked in behind him. He turned to greet the person—a young guy with a toddler in tow.

"Do you guys have snacks? We didn't get to the store yet," the man asked.

"Yep, follow me." Bill walked to the counter and motioned to Gabe. "He can take your order right here." He bent down to the little girl who was still in her pajamas and clutching a teddy bear tight in one fist. "Do you like milk, sweetie, or some juice? And I have muffins—blueberry or banana?"

"Nana!" the little girl squealed and looked up at her daddy. "Okay, Daddy?"

"Yes, that's fine." He turned to Gabe. "A milk for her and a coffee—black—for me."

"Sounds like it might have been a long drive or a long first night," Bill said as he took off the cloche from the muffin stand and snagged a banana one with tongs.

Gabe poured the tired dad a cup of their stiffest brew and snapped on the lid. "Here you go. Sugar and cream are over there if you need it."

The man shook his head. "Gotta have the full test without any impediments to keep up with this one." He tilted his head to his little girl, who Bill now sat beside at the table watching her tear apart the muffin. "You might do better if you put down Teddy."

The girl gave her father a scowl, but then pushed Teddy at Bill. He took the stuffed toy with a smile and pushed the plate closer. "She is a sweetie."

The dad laughed. "Once she'd had her breakfast. Don't distract the nice man from his work, honey."

"Nonsense," Bill said. "This little one is just what the doctor ordered for me today. A little ray of sunshine."

Gabe knew Bill had never had any children. They'd not talked about it much, just enough to know he loved kids but never had any of his own. Bill and Gladys helped with the children's church at Cape Hatteras Baptist and with a kids' lunch program in town. And any time kids came into the shop, he'd drop everything to dote on them.

The little girl shoved a bit of muffin toward her mouth, but half of it ended up on the floor. She scowled as she peered at the ruined pieces, and Bill laughed.

"Just ignore that part, Ellie. Eat the rest," her dad told her.

Gabe started at the girl's name. He knew the name was a popular one, but his heart ached just the same. He wondered where he'd stored their picture albums—photos of Ellie at every stage of life and some of himself. *In those boxes, maybe?*

*Four days to go.*

The doorbell chimed again, and Gabe looked up to see Nora from the beach standing in the doorway. For an instant, Gabe envisioned Ellie and fought hard to find his breath. He noticed the woman's brown hair, tied up in two messy buns, one on either side of her head.

"Fancy seeing you here," she said as she entered.

Bill turned to Gabe and raised an eyebrow.

Gabe looked away from his friend and cleared his throat. "Good morning. What can I get you?"

Nora looked at the board above the counter and cocked a hip. She had on loose shorts today and a T-shirt that read *Coffee, Beach, Sleep, Repeat.* Ellie had hated coffee. Preferred tea. And she hated naps too. Even on vacation.

Why did he keep comparing Nora to his wife? She was obviously much younger as well.

"I think I'll go with the caffe latte, double shot, almond milk, please. To go." She rummaged in the Coach purse hanging from her wrist as Gabe turned to fill her order. "I didn't realize you worked here."

Gabe looked over his shoulder and said, "One of my jobs."

She stopped digging in her purse and looked up at him with wide eyes. "You work more than one job while living at the beach?"

"He does. And he doesn't have a life other than that."

Gabe scowled at Bill as he poured the foam on Nora's drink. "Be quiet, you." He handed Nora her drink and offered a smile. "He's just a senile old man."

She laughed, and he studied her face, not so much like his wife's up close, but still enough to cause his heart to ache. She looked down at the drink and then brought it to her lips. As she sipped, she looked into his eyes. He fought the urge to look away.

"Hmm," she said, closing her eyes. "Very good. And just what I needed." She turned to the father and child. "Morning."

The child buried her head into Bill's shoulder, and he chuckled. "So, you're only friendly with people who give you food, huh?"

"That seems about right," said the dad. "Come on, sweetie. Let's get back to Mommy. Oh! Shoot ... I need another coffee." He turned to Gabe. "Gees, I would be in deep water if I forgot my wife's coffee. Hazelnut cappuccino, please."

Gabe turned to make the drink as Nora began chatting with the father.

"Where are you guys from?"

"Atlanta. We used to come every summer, but this is her first time." He tilted his head to his daughter as she shoved the last bit of muffin into her already bulging cheeks. "Sweetie, can you get a napkin and wipe off your chin? And say goodbye to the nice man."

The little girl pouted but did as she was told, giving Bill a big hug. The old man accepted it with relish, closing his eyes and pulling her in close. "Bye, little one. I hope to see you again."

"Can we, Daddy?" Her little eyes looked up expectantly.

Her dad laughed. "Yep, I think you'll be seeing us regularly this week."

Gabe handed the man his wife's drink, and the duo shuffled out of the shop. Gabe turned his gaze back to Nora.

"Got big plans for the day?"

"Nope," she said, taking another sip of her drink. When she'd given it as much praise as the first sip, she said, "Beach time, baby. Every day. You should come out again. Bring that beautiful pup with you."

Bill began cleaning off the table where the child had been sitting and flashed Gabe another raised eyebrow. "Yeah, buddy, get out and enjoy that sun."

Gabe shook his head. "Thanks, but when I leave here, I'll go to my other job. Sadly, I'm not on vacation."

Bill glowered at him as he passed on his way back to the kitchen, but Gabe kept his focus on Nora. She was the customer after all.

"Shame. I would really like to see that dog again." She smiled, and Gabe chastised himself when he smiled back.

"I got some really good pics of her the other day. I'd love to get more." When Gabe didn't reply, she took another sip of her coffee, then said, "Okay. Gotta go. The sun doesn't wait." She waved a quick goodbye and was out the door.

"What, the what, was that? Or rather who?" Bill sidled up beside him at the counter and nudged his shoulder.

"Someone I met on the beach yesterday. A tourist." Gabe turned and began cleaning out the machine. More customers would be coming, he was sure, and they needed to be ready.

"Hmm. She seems nice. Does she have a husband?"

"I don't know. Don't even know where she's from. She saw Daisy and wanted to pet her. I let her. That's it."

"She took pictures of her."

"Yeah, she had a camera."

Bill leaned against the counter and said, "But you like her. Or like the looks of her."

Gabe couldn't tell Bill she reminded him of Ellie—mainly because she really looked nothing like her. Except for the brown hair, black bathing suit, and fondness for dogs. The man would think he was nuts. Mental. Maybe he was. Maybe every woman would remind him of her now. The only photos he had in the apartment were of Ellie. He worried he'd forget what she looked like or that she'd fade from his memory. He never wanted that to happen. He needed to keep her image alive if nothing else.

"She was a bit chatty, so I chatted. That's all." Gabe knew Bill could see through him even after only knowing him six short months. Perhaps everyone who had ever felt grief could recognize it in others.

But why did he feel drawn to this woman? No matter what he said to Bill or fought in his own mind, there was something there. And he didn't like whatever it was.

## Chapter Eleven

Later that day at the Food Lion, Gabe stocked soda packs while hordes of tourists walked around him. He'd barely put one pack of Pepsi out when it had been snatched off the shelf. He stewed at people's lack of respect. One man had nearly knocked over his whole display trying to get the last case of Diet Coke. Maybe he would ask Brent if he could take a later shift. That way he'd be away from people. But how would he go from that straight to the coffee shop each morning?

He bent down to start a new stack, praying maybe one display would fall on him and end this whole ordeal.

"Gabe! Fancy seeing you twice in one day."

He turned to see Nora hovering over him. From this vantage point, she looked even more like Ellie than before. Her hair lay across her shoulders and was backlit by the fluorescent lighting in the store.

"Hey," he said as he stood. "Thought you were spending all day on the beach."

"Gotta eat sometime," she said. "I was looking for seltzer. Do you guys carry that?"

Once more, a similarity to Ellie. She never drank soda, but sometimes wanted the bubbles.

"I try to not drink caffeine after noon, but water is so boring. Ya know?"

He did know. Ellie had been the same way. When she hit forty, she'd given up caffeine entirely, saying it made her heart flutter. He'd teased her that he'd hoped he was the only thing that caused her heart to dance. She'd leaned in then and kissed him on the cheek.

"Gabe?"

Nora's hand on his arm brought him back to the present. "Sorry. Must need some caffeine myself." He smiled and then pointed. "Seltzer is in this aisle. We've a bunch of flavors too."

She bent her head to the side to look. "Thanks. Hey, I've been invited to a bonfire on the beach tomorrow night. Have you ever done that?"

He shook his head. Why was he finding it so hard to concentrate?

"Would you want to go with me?" At his wide eyes, she was quick to add. "I came alone to the beach but met some new folks today, and they invited me. But I don't know them yet and ... well, I feel like I do know you."

"But you don't," he said.

She looked at her feet. "Yeah. I guess ... we just seemed to click, you know?" When Gabe didn't respond, she added, "You're right. Forget I asked." She began to move her cart away, and Gabe stopped it with his hand.

"What time and where?"

That night, after his shift ended, Gabe returned home with an armload of groceries and two more six packs of beer. Daisy greeted him at the door in her normal butt-wagging mode.

"Yes, get down. You can't have your food if you don't let me in the door."

Daisy immediately moved to the corner of the rug and sat, stuffed toy in her mouth.

"Good girl." Gabe moved to the kitchen and put away the groceries, taking the deli sandwich he'd bought and a bottle of beer back to the couch. When Daisy looked at him with mournful eyes, he said, "Oh right. Sorry." He went back into the kitchen and dumped some kibble in her bowl. After their food routine, Daisy dropped the rhino toy and began to chow down, and Gabe returned to the living room.

When he'd finished his sandwich, he pulled his computer onto his lap and opened the file marked "Us."

He scrolled through file after file until he found a folder marked "That First Year."

Clicking open one of the files within, he started to read.

> Gabe,
> It was really nice to meet you this past weekend. Our conversation was … nice. And I've been thinking about it ever since. Your aunt gave me your email and said I should write. Maybe start up a friendship? Because we had such great conversation, I mean. So … if you're interested, email me back and we can chat.
> Ellie

He'd been interested. He'd emailed her back almost immediately. And he'd found her boldness to be … different, endearing. He'd always been the one going after the girl, but this one came after him.

Like Nora—bold, coming to him first.

He shook his head. He wasn't ready for any kind of relationship—or even a one-night stand or even a date. He thought again about Brent and the young girls and shuddered. In fact, he would never be ready. He turned back to Ellie's emails and drained his bottle of beer.

They had been cautious at first, just building a friendship. He lived in another state at the time, and neither of them thought a relationship would work.

"But God had different plans," Ellie had always said when telling folks about how they met.

Within a year, Gabe had switched jobs and moved. Within two years, they had been engaged. Within three, married. Some people thought they had taken it too slow, but both he and Ellie knew slow was the right pace. They had both been hurt deeply before. Although they both felt God's leading in the relationship, they had both wanted to be sure.

Gabe got up to grab another beer, then returned to his chair. He clicked another file further down in the folder.

> Babe,
> I plan to come up to you this Friday. I'll be there by the time you get home from work. What do you want to do this weekend?
> Gabe

He smiled, then took another swig of beer. He'd actually gone up even earlier and had surprised her at work that time with flowers in hand. He'd loved making her coworkers jealous and making her feel special. They had gone to a nice dinner and then spent the evening on her too-small couch watching television. The simple things in life meant the most to them.

After they had been married a few years, Ellie complained of not getting flowers as much as when they had first dated. But they also exacerbated her allergies, so Gabe had cut back. Now he felt bad for not showering her with flowers every day of her life despite the allergies.

He thought then of the funeral flowers that had surrounded her small box of remains. Taking another swig of his beer, he clicked into another folder.

> My love,
> Remember that time we rented a two-person kayak? What a disaster. I think we were engaged by then, but I think your sister thought we couldn't make it after we came back from our jaunt with me sulking in the boat and you pulling it along from the water. LOL

Gabe remembered well. It had been here in the Outer Banks, on the bay side. Ellie and his sister, Cameron, thought it would be fun to kayak together with their boyfriends. Cameron and her beau at the time had enjoyed a lovely afternoon around the bay. Gabe and Ellie had fought almost from the beginning.

"You need to steer," he'd told her.

"But I'm in the front. And why can't we just paddle normally?"

"Because we each only have one paddle. And since you're in the front, you do the steering."

Ellie had remained silent for a moment as they fought their kayak, going nowhere.

"But isn't a rudder at the back?" she asked. "That means you would be steering."

Gabe watched as his sister and her boyfriend had moved gracefully away, seemingly without any issues. But he and Ellie had gotten into their first real fight. When Gabe couldn't reason with her anymore and when they couldn't even get back to shore because of their lack of cooperation, he'd jumped out of the kayak and pulled it to shore. His sister and her boyfriend had watched in horror.

> I can still remember your face when you later learned I WAS right. YOU should have been steering.

He shook her voice from his head and took another swallow of beer.

Ellie loved to be right, and she often was, which both irritated Gabe and made her more endearing. She often thought herself as stupid, but she was a lot smarter than she gave herself credit for.

As he swallowed the last of his beer, he thought back to Nora's invitation today. Why had he agreed to join her tomorrow night? There was something about her ... was it simply that she reminded him of Ellie? Or was there something more. He snapped the laptop shut and closed his eyes.

"God, I don't know what you're doing." He'd not talked to God in quite some time, but he felt lost from his moorings and needed guidance. "I know we've not chatted in a while, but I think I'm lost, and I need help. I miss Ellie so much I'm seeing her in other people. I don't think I can do this life without her. And yet, I'm not ready to let others in. What the hell am I doing? Care to give any help?"

He felt God had been silent for far too long.

*You know that isn't the case, babe. God is always right beside you. You're the one who has remained silent, distant from God.*

"Gee, God, you sound an awful lot like my dead wife."

Daisy came over then and laid her head on his knee. He wiped away a tear and scratched her nose. "I'm okay, girl."

Now, if only he could believe his own words.

## Chapter Twelve

The next day, Gabe was in the coffee shop well ahead of Bill and had brought Daisy along as the older man had suggested. He positioned her bed in the back corner so as not to be in the way and directed her to lie there and be quiet. She obeyed until Bill and Gladys entered.

"Hey, girl! How are you?" Bill exclaimed as Daisy's butt nearly wagged off her body.

"What brings you here, little lady?" Gladys looked at Gabe with a smile.

"Bill said to bring her, so I did. She misses being around people. I hope that's okay."

Gladys dropped a basket full of pastries on the counter, then gave Gabe a hug. "Of course! Bill says she's a good little girl, and the customers will love it." She turned back to her goodies and began arranging them on some pretty plates.

"You need to bring her everywhere," Bill said as he squatted down to pet Daisy. "She's a good dog. In fact, bring her over for dinner anytime. If she gets along with cats, that is. She seems to be getting to know them right now." Bill laughed as the dog sniffed hard at his leg, then moved on to lick his face. "I'm sure Gladys would fill her belly and yours. Okay, Daisy. I think my face is sufficiently washed now. I better go help your dad."

Gabe helped Gladys by adding some tongs to her pastry stacks and shuddered. "I never liked when Ellie called me that."

"What? Dad?" Bill tied on his apron and went to refill the sugar. "I know you didn't have kids, but do you really hate the idea that much?"

"Yeah. I mean, no, not that part. But she is a dog, not a kid."

"So? Don't you feed her and take care of her and love her? Don't you want to ensure she has a good life?"

Gabe shrugged. "I guess so."

Gladys stepped back, pleased with her display and then turned to Gabe. "Our heavenly Father wants those things for us even though he isn't *technically* our real father. People call him Daddy."

"Yeah." Gabe shuddered. "That's kind of weird too. I don't think of him as that kind of father."

"Why not?" Bill came around behind the counter then and leaned against it. "Do you take him your stress and pain? Do you wish you could crawl up on his lap and cry? Isn't that the same as a daddy?"

"I guess so. I never thought of it that way." Gabe turned to the coffeepot and began pouring in grounds. Too late, he realized he'd forgotten the filter. Instead of getting upset, he just started cleaning out the grounds to try again. He'd read once in a book it's what men do—keep their emotions in check and solve the problem.

Bill placed his hand on Gabe's shoulder. "Have you been keeping up your relationship with God? It's so important, especially when we're grieving."

Gabe shrugged off Bill's hand and finished cleaning up the rest of the spilled grounds. When he'd done the best he could do, he pushed in a filter and started again. "Yeah, I talk to him." The answer wasn't completely a lie since he had technically offered up a prayer just last night. "I'm not sure he's listening anymore, though." Gabe pressed the on button and then grabbed the broom. He wanted to get away from their religious talk. Couldn't they just let it alone?

As he was walking toward the front, he paused and turned back to the couple. "Hey, why are you here this morning anyway, Gladys? You don't normally grace us with your presence."

She smiled and patted Bill on the cheek. "Somebody forgot to pay some bills, so I'm going to go through that muddled space he calls an office and make sure nothing else gets missed."

Bill frowned and said, "Hey, I can't keep everything straight. And that's why I'm going to let Gladys start helping more."

Gabe chuckled a bit to himself as he recognized the rote tone of Bill's response.

*Happy wife, happy life—right, babe?*

Nodding, Gabe pushed through the front door and out to the porch. The sun was just beginning to rise above the rental homes, and Gabe could smell the fresh sea air. He inhaled and held it for a beat before blowing it out again.

He missed sharing the duties of life with someone and was glad Gladys had convinced Bill to share the load. Gabe had helped Ellie with her business and had always felt closer to her as a result. And he knew what a mess Bill's desk was. He could only imagine what might lie underneath all the papers and stacks of magazines in there.

Bill was not wrong about something else—Gabe did need to be closer to the Lord again. But since God had taken Ellie from him—even though Gabe knew that was not really how it worked—he'd had a hard time sinking back into his faith.

*Three days to go.*

"God," he said to the sky, "I'm sorry for straying. I would like to start talking more. To understand you better. To get to know you as a father again. To heal from this grief. But I don't know where to start."

A customer pulled into the driveway, and Gabe resumed his sweeping. A few minutes later, three more cars had arrived, and Gabe hurried inside to help Bill.

The morning flew by with a slew of orders and new people. Gabe wished they had more regulars. Perhaps then he would feel more grounded in this place. Maybe he'd be able to call it home if he knew more people.

Gladys had helped when business surged but had gone home about an hour ago with a large stack of papers to "put things to rights" at her own desk.

When lunchtime neared, the crowds had finally died down. Gabe took a cloth out to wipe down the table. Daisy had collapsed back in her bed, a long morning of greeting every single customer and making them feel special under her belt.

As Bill was wiping down the counter, Gabe said, "That girl invited me to a bonfire tonight."

"What girl?" Bill looked up and frowned. "Oh! The one from yesterday? What was her name?"

"Nora. Yeah. I guess she's alone and asked me to go." He pushed the chairs under the table and began rearranging the newspapers laid on top.

"Like a date?"

"I think more like security. I guess because I live here, she thinks I'm a safe stranger." Gabe shrugged his shoulders and threw the washrag back into his bucket. "And it might be nice to meet some new people."

Bill fixated on his counter, wiping for a minute before saying, "But they aren't staying, Gabe. They're temporary friends at best. Why don't you come over for dinner tonight. I know Gladys would love it. She said as much before she left."

Gabe could hear the hurt in his friend's tone. Bill had invited Gabe time and time again to his home and to his church, but Gabe had always declined. Yet, he felt the urge to go to this bonfire with this stranger. To get back out into the world a bit. Ellie had always been the one to push him into new things and meet new people. Despite being an introvert herself, she longed to be loved by others and had a heart to love them back.

"God wants us to share his love, Gabe," she'd told him once. "Even if some people are hard to love, it's God's commission. If we don't meet new people, how can we tell them about Christ and his salvation?"

Gabe knew she was right, but he'd never felt like an evangelizer. He'd tried his best, knew how to turn that personality switch to "on" for certain events. But after any party or social event, he'd always felt so drained.

Something about meeting up with Nora felt less draining than spending a night with Bill and his wife.

He turned back to his new friend now—he could call Bill his friend, and he'd work harder to include him in his life. "It's just something I think I want to do, Bill."

When the older man looked away and kept tidying things that didn't need tidying, Gabe put a tentative hand on his shoulder. "Could you ask Gladys if she would feel up to making me something healthy this week? I have Thursday off from the store, and I'm getting a little sick of those bland noodles."

Bill turned to him and offered a small smile. "You don't have to do that. I know we're old, and you would rather spend time with someone your own age."

Gabe shook his head. "Ellie and I never worried about that kind of thing. We had friends of all ages. It's just ..." He stepped back and sighed. "I'm out of my socializing routine. And maybe I worry you will think differently once you see me out of this element." He gestured at the coffee makers, counters, and sugar table. "I'm not the ball of laughs I am here, you know."

Bill scowled. "You barely crack a smile in this place. Sometimes, I think you would rather be scraping crap off those boats in the harbor."

"Wait ... is that an option? Do you know someone I could ask about that? Would I have to deal with customers?" Gabe tapped his finger against his chin. "That is a good idea. Yeah, think I might walk down there later and inquire."

Bill snapped him with his towel. "Okay, okay. I get it."

Gabe laughed. "No, listen. It's ... This lady is only here for the week. If she doesn't think that highly of me, it won't matter. If I lose my standing in your eyes, what would I have left?"

"I already don't think that highly of you, so how could it dip too much?" The glint in Bill's eyes indicated he teased, and then he punched Gabe in the shoulder and laughed. "I get it. I'll see what Gladys can whip up. You plan to be at our house Thursday night. And"—he pointed a finger at Gabe—"No backing out."

Gabe made an X across his chest with a finger and said, "Promise."

## Chapter Thirteen

After Gabe finished his shift at the Food Lion, he ran home to get ready for the bonfire. He'd not felt this nervous about anything in a long time. Picking through his closet, he remembered how Ellie used to try on a variety of outfits before heading out to a fun function.

"What about this one?" she would ask.

She looked great in almost everything—even the baggy sweatpants and hooded sweatshirts she wore most winter days. When she really tried to look nice, she did so easily. But she never thought her wardrobe—or she—was good enough.

"You look great," he'd tell her. "We've got to get going soon."

"I know." She'd walk past him and into the other room where they had a full-length mirror. After inspecting herself for a few seconds, she'd return to their bedroom, pulling off at least one item.

"Why do you ask if you never believe me?"

She'd smile and say, "It isn't right. Give me one second."

She was never late—he'd admired her for that—but he wished she'd have seen her own inner beauty. What she wore on the outside rarely mattered. Gabe knew from the many people who had attended her funeral that the color of her shoes had never made an impact on them. But her big heart had.

"Right. So why do I care about what I'm wearing. Take your own advice, Gabe."

He pulled on a pair of jeans and a red polo, then grabbed a hooded sweatshirt in case the night grew cold—which it had been this late into the season—and a blanket. Daisy stood by watching his activities, stuffed toy in her mouth and familiar forlorn look in her eyes.

"Yes, I'm going out. You've had me to yourself every night since we've moved here. You'll get over it." He squatted down to pet her head, and she dropped the toy long enough to give him several licks across the face. "Thank you. Now no other dog will want me. And I promise to come back to you soon."

He stood again and considered if he should use some mouthwash. But this was not a date, right? A flash of times past went through his thoughts of the days when he and Ellie dated. They would spend the weekend together—in separate bedrooms—and then go home on Sunday. Late every Sunday, when he would have to make his way home, he'd said, "I promise to come back to you soon."

He shook his head of the thoughts and stood. After one last check in the same full-length mirror Ellie had consulted so many times, he changed his polo to a T-shirt instead that read *My parents said I could be whatever I wanted so I decided to be awesome*, then headed for the door.

The sun had all but left the sky already as Gabe made his way to the beach. Nora had told him the bonfire would be south of the shop, so he crossed over the dune and took a right. He saw the beginnings of a blaze ahead and made

*Changing Tides*

his way in that direction, hoping he'd recognize Nora in the waning light.

As he neared the fire, he saw several people poking at the fire and holding cans—he was hoping beer. Nora stood on the other side of the flames, chatting and laughing with another woman.

Gabe wondered for a moment how old Nora was. He'd never been good at determining that, and how did you politely ask someone—especially a woman—her age.

*She isn't staying, Gabe,* he heard Bill's voice in his head.

*Right. Her age doesn't matter. She isn't staying. This is just an experiment.*

Gabe slowed as he neared the group, and Nora looked up. She smiled and waved him closer. He came around the group to stand beside her.

"Hey. I'm glad you came." She gave his hand a squeeze and then pointed at her friend. "This is Melanie ... Mel. She's here from Alabama."

"Hi! Nora told me you might come. The more the merrier! We love meeting people on our trips."

Melanie had long blonde hair and red-tinged blue eyes. Gabe guessed she either had not slept well or had been day drinking. Maybe she just woke from a nap.

"Mel and her husband"—Nora pointed to a bearded man on the other side of the fire—"travel all over the US."

"Jack," the man said, leaning over the fire to shake Gabe's hand. "Nice to meet ya."

"And sometimes abroad," Mel said with a smile. "We just came back from Greece." She flipped her hair over her shoulder, then pulled at the hem of her shirt. Maybe she was as nervous around strangers as he was.

Jack introduced another couple and a few other single women around the fire. Most of them didn't give Gabe a second look, and he felt fine with that.

Ellie had always wanted to go to Greece. Another way he'd failed her. *Why didn't I ever take her to Greece?* Gabe knew—his job. He'd always been so caught up in working and saving money for their retirement. What a joke that turned out to be. Now there would be no need for lots of funds in their—his—retirement.

"Gabe?" Nora's voice brought him back to the present. He turned to her. "I asked if you'd like a drink."

"We have a variety of beers," Mel said, moving closer to a cooler wedged into the sand. "Lots of IPAs and some domestics if you're not into the microbrew kind of thing."

"An IPA is great, actually," Gabe told her. He took the one she handed him and tried to read the label in the dim light.

"It's not from OBX but is from North Carolina. Although, have you been to any of the brewery places here on the island?" Melanie took a sip from her own can and raised her eyebrows at Gabe.

He shook his head. "No. I spend most of my time working."

She nodded but then turned wide eyes to Nora. Gabe could tell she was not impressed. Ellie had always called him a workaholic—not something he'd taken as a negative. After all, you had to work to pay for things. And he'd been socking money away to move them south. To make all of Ellie's dreams come true.

He took a swallow of the beer to chase down the grief. Nora sidled closer to him.

"Don't mind her. We just met so it's not like we're besties or anything." She gazed into the fire a minute before saying, "She is fun, though."

She turned to him and smiled, and he felt his heart skip a beat. He and Ellie had always made fun of those sappy romance novels where the author said that, but he really felt it. Instantly, he also felt guilt. He'd never had that feeling with anyone other than Ellie. How could he possibly betray her this way? He took another swallow of his beer and looked away from Nora out at the surf.

"So what do you do?" Melanie's husband—what had Nora said his name was?—called from across the fire as he poked the kindling with a stick.

"I work part-time at the coffee shop right out from here and part-time at the Food Lion."

"And the rest of the time on the beach, heh?" The man smiled and nudged the man sitting next to him. "Must be nice living the vacation life all year round."

"I've only been here six months, so I couldn't say."

The man stared at him for a moment, and then smiled again. "See any hurricanes yet?"

Gabe wondered if he'd been this shallow as a tourist. The people here had lives just like everywhere else. But visitors seemed to think life here was all about sunbathing and hurricanes.

"Not really hurricane season yet. Although I hear there's one off to the south of us."

The man's eyes grew large, and he turned to his friend—forgetting Gabe for the time being.

"A hurricane?" said Mel, still beside him. "It won't affect us, will it?"

Gabe shook his head. "It's pretty far out. Probably won't even make land. No worries."

"Phew!" Mel sagged against Nora for a moment and smiled. "Would hate to have to repack all that crap I just unpacked."

She turned to another woman, and Gabe felt relieved the conversation had moved on from him. He'd grown more introverted since moving here ... since Ellie had died.

He glanced at Nora from the corner of his eye, but she stared into the fire as if not noticing him or the conversations going on around her.

"Nice night," he said. When feeling uncomfortable, the weather was always a safe conversation. He wiped at the condensation on his can and then took a swig. Bitter, but not bad.

"Yes." She turned to him and smiled. "There's a hammock at my rental, and I watch the sun rise every morning from it. It's so peaceful here."

Gabe wondered briefly if her rental was the one they had stayed at a few years ago with the hammock Ellie had loved so much. "Only at the beachside rentals," he said, instantly regretting being negative.

"What do you mean? You don't think it's peaceful here?"

He took another sip of his beer as he thought how best to explain. And if he should. He didn't want to bring her down or squash her perfect vacation. Maybe it was his own need to have someone on the same plane as him. Someone who was equally miserable. But why would he want to do that to her? She was on vacation.

"It's just …" He struggled a moment with how to spin the facts, so they were not as negative. "The waves and the dunes kind of create a sound barrier on this side. Once you're more inland—even though there isn't much inland here—the noise of daily life comes back." There, he'd said it. He'd held these delusions once too that the beach was more calming because of the lack of noise. It *did* have a lack of noise because the homes were strategically placed to face the beach. And the dunes buffeted the sound. This not only helped tourists enjoy the views, but also blocked out noise—except for the sound of the waves crashing, of course.

When he looked at Nora's frowning face, he internally cursed his negative spirit.

"Sorry. It is lovely here. I didn't mean to ruin it for you."

Nora's face cleared, and she shrugged. "I guess you're right. But vacations are all about the mystery and the mystique of a foreign place, right? I'll forgive you, but you might want to work on your conversation skills when talking with other tourists."

He laughed and agreed, although he didn't plan to make friends with many tourists. Did he intend to make friends at all? He wondered again what he was doing in this place. What was his life to be now? Where did he go next?

"Maybe that's what happens with conch shells." At his blank stare, she continued. "You know. How you put it up to your ear and hear the surf?"

He nodded. "Maybe. In reverse, though, I think?"

She shrugged and introduced him to a few more people before suggesting they put down their blankets. Gabe spread hers for her—a buffalo check plaid—and put his down. It was an old army blanket that had belonged to Ellie's dad. Gabe had softer blankets somewhere but had yet to unpack them, and this one reminded him of Ellie. He thought again of those boxes in his bedroom closet. He should really unpack those.

They settled down on the blankets next to the fire.

Gabe stared into the flames as conversations took place all around him. The group joked about sunburns and lamented over the long drives to get here. Gabe even chimed in a couple of times with some tips on avoiding sunburn. Even though the conversation was lively and Nora's company enjoyable, Gabe fought the nagging urge to return home. He found himself putting on that persona that Ellie had hated so much.

"You always act like a different person when we're around others. Why can't you be yourself? You're pretty great, you know. Let others see that."

But he used that persona as a shield. He'd never really wanted people—other than Ellie—in his life. He called himself an extroverted introvert. He could act social and outgoing when needed but wanted mainly to be by himself.

But this was more than his introverted tendencies tonight. He continued to feel the ongoing guilt of betraying Ellie.

*But I'm not here for romantic reasons. I just wanted to break out of my normal routine.*

Still, he couldn't help feeling like Ellie would be upset.

"I'm not one of those women who say, 'Find yourself a new mate after I'm gone,'" she'd told him once. "You're mine and always mine."

He'd agreed. "When you're gone, I'll not want anyone else." He'd pulled her into his embrace and nibbled on her neck. "It was hard enough training you."

They had laughed and snuggled on the couch together, as was their norm. He'd felt safe with Ellie. Home. Content. Now he felt as adrift as the shells and seaweed he saw littering the sand beside him. He grabbed another beer and quickly downed half.

"So why did you move to Avon," Nora asked, breaking him once again from his reverie. He really needed to focus better on the conversation.

"Well, after my wife died ..." He swallowed the lump in his throat. "... I kind of didn't have a sense of direction anymore, you know." Nora nodded as if she did, indeed, understand. "Ellie had always wanted to move to the beach. But we had decided ... no, I guess I decided we needed to wait until I retired. She worked from home as a freelancer, so I brought in the bulk of our funds." Why was Gabe telling this stranger all his baggage? He didn't know, but it also felt good to talk it out. "Anyway ... we put it off. And then she got cancer—" He choked on the emotion and crushed his now empty can. He stood from the blanket and walked to the cooler. He threw the empty can in a trash bag and picked a domestic this time. He turned and walked a few paces away from the fire circle.

Nora rose too and came to his side. Placing her hand on his shoulder, she said, "Let's take a walk."

He agreed. Nora offered an explanation to the group, and followed Gabe as he drifted toward the shore.

The tide coming in and out created a balance to Gabe's emotions.

"So what's your story?" He turned back to Nora and noticed she was holding her arms tight against her chest. "Cold?"

She nodded, and he pulled his sweatshirt off and handed it to her.

"Thanks." She pulled it on and untied her ponytail, shaking out her hair.

As it fell around her shoulders Gabe considered her once more. What had he seen that reminded him so much of Ellie? They both had brown hair, but Nora's—he now noticed—was straight where Ellie's had been curly. Something she both loved and hated about herself. She'd tried to grow her hair long several times, hoping it would straighten out more as it grew. But she'd been disappointed time and again when it simply seemed to grow outward with thickness instead.

Nora was thinner ... much thinner. Almost sickly thin, he realized.

He focused on her again. "So? Not going to tell me your story?"

She smiled. "I needed to get away is all. Kind of like you, I guess. Except I can only stay a week."

Gabe's heart lurched then. A week. Why was he even getting involved at all with someone who couldn't stay? *Was* he getting involved?

"But I'm glad I met you," she said, turning to look into his eyes. "And those folks back there." She thumbed over her shoulder. "I wanted to be alone this week, but I guess God had different plans. And I'm glad for it."

God's plans. That had been exactly what Ellie had told people about how they had met—God had different plans. Right. Gabe had not thought much about God's plans since he'd taken Ellie from him too soon. Instead, he'd made his own plans, devised his own life map, and never consulted his Lord and Savior.

"God and I don't talk too much anymore. I'm not sure what he wants for me these days." He took another gulp of his beer.

"Even amid my own troubles, I know God has a plan. God *always* has a plan, Gabe. Don't you believe that? I almost have to sometimes. It's the only thing that keeps me going."

He had to look at Nora now to ensure she wasn't really Ellie standing beside him. His wife had said something almost exactly the same all the time. They even had a small sign hanging in their kitchen with that sentiment—God has a plan.

He inhaled the salty air and shivered against the cool breeze. "Except it's hard to figure out what that plan is. When Ellie got sick, I cursed him pretty hard. I know the story is cliché, but it hurt. We didn't marry until we were in our thirties—we didn't have that many years together. I felt —*feel* robbed. And I have no clue what God wants me to do now. When I married Ellie, I had a purpose—to be a good husband. Now what do I do?"

Nora stepped up beside him and pushed her toes into the sand. "I agree. The road ahead isn't always clear." She turned to him. "Are you doing what you think Ellie would want?"

"She wanted to move to the beach, so yeah. This is the life she wanted to be living."

"But is it the life she'd want you to live now?"

Gabe stared off to the darkened horizon where a ship's lights blinked off and on. The light felt like something within his brain trying to find purchase but unable to.

"I bet Ellie thought her purpose was to be a good wife, right? Just like your purpose. Speaking from the female perspective, I bet she worked hard every day to please you. That was her main goal." Nora sat down in the damp sand and looked up at him. "I bet she sacrificed many things to ensure your happiness, just like you tried to do for her. And I think she would want you to be happy even without her."

Gabe looked down at her and frowned. But had he made Ellie happy? And was it too late? He shook his head. *Of course* it was too late.

"Sheesh, this sand is cold. Help me up?" Nora held out a hand to him, and he took it, lifting her up off the beach. Nora brushed off her backside and smiled. "I think I'd like to get back to the fire. You coming?"

"I think I'll stay here for a bit and then head home if you're okay with that. I'm suddenly not feeling very social."

Nora nodded and pulled off his shirt. "I'll be warm once I get back to the fire. See you tomorrow?"

He nodded and said, "I'm sorry I haven't been much of a buffer tonight. Are you sure you feel okay with these folks?"

"Yeah." She looked out at the rolling waves and said, "I kind of lied to get you here. I guess I thought maybe you might need a night away too." She turned back to him and gave him a smile. "I think I was right, and I'm glad you came." She moved away, back to her other new friends.

Gabe watched her go for a moment before pulling on his sweatshirt again and inhaling her perfume. Tears came unbidden to his eyes, and he sat down with a thud on the beach.

"What do you want, God? I feel so lost now. So rudderless. I thought maybe you wanted me to get back out into the dating scene, but this isn't for me. I don't want anyone but Ellie." He picked up a fistful of sand and let it drip through his fingers. Then he looked out again to the distant horizon. "That light blinking out there is like my thoughts—sharp and in focus one minute, struggling to stay lit the next. Lord, I need your guidance. Please." He put his head in his hands and wept.

## Chapter Fourteen

Gabe groaned when Daisy nudged his head and began licking his face the next morning. After a fitful night's sleep and crying out from several vivid dreams of Ellie, Daisy had whined so loudly at Gabe's distress that he'd let her in and invited her up on the bed—something he and Ellie had never allowed before.

He yelled for Daisy to stop her relentless licking and turned his face to the pillow, unready to rise. When Daisy laid her head on his and began to whine, he threw off the covers and put his feet on the floor. He'd asked Bill for the next three days off, but Daisy still needed her routine.

*Two days to go.*

After throwing on a pair of sweats and sweatshirt, Gabe leashed up Daisy and took her on their daily walk. They traversed the familiar path, but Gabe now looked more at his surroundings. Up ahead, some kids gathered for the bus. At the local realty agency, a man put out the open flag. The island was coming to life at a time he didn't normally see, and he felt a renewed sense of awe about this island life. He thought of the stickers he'd seen—"Salt Life." And "Everything's better at the beach." Was it? Did he feel the "salt life"? What did that even mean?

He thought about what the Bible said about living a salty life. He didn't think that's what the bumper stickers and T-shirts meant, though. He thought the verse was in Matthew or maybe Luke. Maybe both, actually. Maybe it was in all the Gospels. Something about being the salt of the earth.

"But if the salt loses its saltiness, how can it be made salty again? It's no longer good for anything." He thought that was at least part of the verse.

Had he lost his saltiness? Had he ever had any? His grandmother was salty—full of piss and vinegar, she'd have said. That sounded like a mixed metaphor, though. He'd once fought for things he believed in. Until the world beat his fervor out of him. Now he went along with the flow, too tired to fight anymore.

He thought back to what Nora had said the night before. Would Ellie want this life for him? They had made wills and planned for where their money would go but not for what they would do without the other.

"I plan to sequester myself after you die," he'd told Ellie once. "I'll become that grumpy old man the neighborhood kids talk about."

He kind of was that grumpy man and sequestered—at least from his friends and family—but he didn't know any neighborhood kids here. Nor did he think they cared—or even noticed—he lived here.

He turned back toward the apartment and had to pull Daisy out of some ornamental grass where she must have smelled some possible prey. Maybe there was a dog park or something where he and Daisy could meet some new people. People who were here to stay.

Was he here to stay?

His phone pinged and he looked at a text from his sister.

**You really need to text me back, big brother. I worry about you down there by yourself.**

He swiped the message away. He knew he'd better touch base with more than a quick email soon, or she'd go to more drastic measures. But he didn't know what to say. In the past, he'd have sent her some funny meme or GIF. The one he liked the most was a dog sitting in a building engulfed in flames and saying, "This is fine." But even that had lost its funny vibe as of late.

As they neared the coffee shop, Gabe had a sudden urge to be with these people he'd met and called his friends. He swung open the back door to the shop, startling Gladys, who was reaching up into a closet for more supplies.

"Oh! Oh, Gabe. How are you, dear?" She put down the pile of napkins she'd been holding and patted his cheek. Then she bent over and patted Daisy's head with the same affection. "Hello, my pretty girl." She turned back to Gabe. "Since you're here, can you reach those stirrers on the top shelf? Bill just ran down to the store for some more milk, and I can't quite reach."

Gabe handed her Daisy's leash and reached on tiptoe for the stirrers.

"Thank you, dear." She exchanged the leash for the supplies. "Now come in here and eat some of these delicious lemon bars I made."

Ellie's favorite. He wondered if Gladys somehow knew. The older woman had tried to mother him since he'd moved here, but he'd avoided her attentions, always using Bill as their buffer. He realized now he'd almost avoided Gladys and wondered why.

His own mother was not the motherly type, always more focused on her own life and worries. When Ellie had died, his parents had not come to the funeral but had sent a simple condolence card and some flowers.

*They're elderly, babe. And the flight is long and tiring. You know that.*

He brushed Ellie's words from his mind. Yes, the travel would have been difficult, but he was their only son. Why couldn't they have made the effort this one time?

He unsnapped Daisy's leash, and she scampered after Gladys into the shop. He wished he could be as easy going as his pup. Maybe that's why Ellie had loved dogs so much—for their unwavering and unconditional love to just about everyone.

Gabe had always been partial to cats. He enjoyed their aloof nature, not needing constant attention the way dogs did.

As if to illustrate his point, Daisy nudged his hand.

"Go lay down. You know the drill."

Daisy slinked away to her bed.

"Oh, you poor thing," Gladys cooed. "I think I have a few pieces of leftover bacon over here. Come, Daisy!"

The hound bounded from her bed to the old woman's side. Gladys laughed when Daisy barely chewed the yummy morsel.

"If you keep feeding her like that, she won't want to leave," Gabe told Gladys. He moved to the fridge and pulled a diet soda from its depths. He thought of how Bill kept them in there just for him. He'd truly made friends here, so why couldn't he let them into his life?

Just then Bill blew in the front door holding a brown bag full of groceries.

"I thought you only needed milk," Gladys said as she helped her husband with the bag. Gabe sensed a bit of tension in her words, but she kissed Bill's cheek and seemed to move past whatever the issue was.

Bill chuckled. "Well, you know I can't resist a deal." He eyed Gabe. "Thought you needed time off."

Gabe shrugged. "Couldn't stay away, I guess."

They moved to the kitchen where Gladys pecked Bill again on the cheek, and he smiled. Gabe fought a moment of raw emotion, wondering if he would ever feel the special bond with a loved one again. And did he even want to?

Bill grabbed a piece of bacon for himself and motioned for Gabe to join him at the front table. Daisy padded after the older man, sniffing at his hand.

"So how was the bonfire?" Bill asked when they were settled.

Gabe shrugged. "Okay. I didn't stay long."

"Was it just the two of you?" Bill moved his eyebrows up and down suggestively.

"No, and stop that. It's not a romantic thing."

"Why not?" Bill slipped Daisy another hunk of bacon then told her to go lie down.

"I'm still mourning Ellie. And I don't care to find another relationship." He watched Bill stir milk into his coffee and whispered, "How long after your wife died until you and Gladys found each other?"

Bill tapped the stirrer against the side of the cup. "About a year, but I had known her previously."

"Ten years," Gladys chimed in from the kitchen. "Ten years we knew each other. We went to the same church, and I knew Phyllis."

Bill nodded. "No need to whisper. Nothing gets past her—right, Gladys?" He winked at Gabe. "God knew all along what was going to happen. And I couldn't be happier." Gladys blew him a kiss from the kitchen.

Gabe wondered what plans God had for him. And would he know if he saw them?

"I think I made a mistake moving here." The revelation startled him as much as it did Bill and Gladys, who came rushing from the kitchen to sit beside him.

"Why do you say that, dear?"

Gabe shrugged. "This was Ellie's dream, not mine. Not really. I mean, I wanted to give it to her but wasn't sure I wanted it for myself, you know?" He shredded a napkin lying on the table. "I miss working with numbers. Did you know I did that?"

Bill nodded, but Gladys shook her head. "You told me," Bill said, "I'd be happy to let you sort out our books. I could use all the help I can get." He glanced at Gladys, and she offered a tight smile.

"I thought Gladys was helping with that?"

Gladys smoothed the expression on her face and said, "I'm sure you'd be better at it, dear."

Once again, Gabe seemed to detect something under the surface of the couple's expressions and sentiments. Unsure, Gabe nodded. "I was a finance guy. Excel spreadsheets. Actuals. That kind of thing. I used to call myself the 'Numbers Monkey'."

"So ... why did you stop?" Gladys rested a wrinkled hand on his.

Gabe's heart swelled at the touch and thought again of his own mother. She rarely touched him except for one hug when she arrived and one hug before she left. But Ellie's mom had been more affectionate, and he realized now he was still dealing with the grief of her dying too. How he longed to let someone in again, to be part of a family. But then his heart lurched, and he shut the door.

"I failed Ellie by working so hard. So, I gave up my career and started fresh the way she wanted to."

"Is that what she really wanted? And she isn't here now, Gabe," Bill said, leaning across the table and adding his hand atop Gladys's. "She would want you to be happy. Don't you think?"

"Nora said the same thing, and now I feel like my whole plan is shifting. I don't know what I want. I always did what Ellie wanted. That was my purpose—to keep her happy. Now what do I do?"

Gladys sat back and shook her head. "No, no, no ... your purpose is *not* to make anyone happy. We must find love and happiness within ourselves." She tapped a finger to her chest. "God gives me my purpose."

There was that name again. God. He thought of his most recent conversations with the elusive God. He'd still not heard any definitive answer.

"Do you still have Bible study tonight at your house?"

Bill glanced at Gladys before saying, "They started a new program at the church, so I go there on Wednesdays now."

Gabe caught the subtle tap Bill put on Gladys's knee. She opened her mouth to speak but quickly shut it, glancing at her husband. A look passed between them that Gabe couldn't read. Probably happy he'd finally come back into the faith or something. Their prayers answered. He scoffed.

Bill jumped up, and Daisy barked, coming to his side. "Get out of here and do some praying until then. I'll swing by for you around five and we can grab some dinner first."

## Chapter Fifteen

Gabe stepped into the foyer of the Cape Hatteras Baptist Church and flinched. *Nope, no lightning.*

Bill slapped him on the back and laughed. "Come on. We meet in this little room over here."

Gabe clutched the Bible he'd dug out of a box. A New American Standard version—he'd used this Bible all through college and most of his adulthood. After he sat down next to Bill in what looked like a classroom, he opened the book and squinted at the text.

"Whew," Bill said over his shoulder. "That is why yours is so small compared to mine." He hefted his tome. "I gotta have the large type."

"Ellie always said that too. And others." He held up the small book. "But this version is straight from God, so I'm not changing."

"I thought the King James version was the one direct from God?"

Gabe winked. "I'm kidding. But I think the Hebrew or Greek would be the one direct, not any of the more modern versions we have today."

Bill laughed. "Well, I'm not learning Hebrew or Greek, so I'll have to work it out and trust God to set me right."

Their conversation died down, and Gabe looked around at the group. Mostly men.

"So, this is a men's group?"

His friend hesitated as his eyes darted around the room but said, "Yes."

Gabe noticed Bill running his hands over his pant legs over and over again and wondered why his friend had suddenly grown so tense. He noticed Bill refused to look at him now too. Was he worried Gabe was going to embarrass him or something?

"Hey." He tapped Bill on the shoulder. "I was kidding earlier. I'll be on my best behavior, I promise."

Bill gave him an odd look and started to say something, but then a man stood in front of the small group gathered. He went around the other side of a lectern at the front of the room.

"That's Pastor Tim," Bill whispered.

"Hello, everyone. I'm glad you all chose to join us tonight."

The man looked like a pastor at Gabe's last church—scruffy bearded with several tattoos and a congenial air. He immediately felt drawn to the man.

"Let's open with a word of prayer. Dear heavenly Father, you know we all come here because we're dealing with some kind of grief—"

Gabe turned quickly to look at Bill, who had clenched his eyes tight in prayer mode.

"A grief group?" Gabe whispered. "You brought me to a grief group?"

Out of the corner of his mouth, Bill whispered back, "We're praying. You can forgive me later."

Exasperated, Gabe considered leaving. But he had no ride home without Bill. He closed his eyes again and listened to the prayer.

"We're so thankful, Father, that you have brought this group together so we might share in our sorrows and find new ways within your Word to cope. May our words be pleasing to you tonight, Lord, and may our hearts be lightened. In your most precious and holy name, amen."

Gabe opened his eyes and fought the urge to bolt. He wanted to be mad at Bill, but also secretly wanted to know if this group could help. Was this God speaking?

"For those new to our group, I'll give a little synopsis about what we do here. First, you don't have to share—"

*Good.*

"Second, whatever you do choose to say in here, stays in here. This is a safe space. Normally, we're a mixed group of people, but I see we're all men tonight. Guess we won't be delving too far into feelings then."

A small spattering of laughter tinkled about the room while Gabe scowled.

"You go to hell for lying, you know," he whispered to Bill.

"Do not. And I didn't lie. We're a men's group. Tonight anyway."

"Bill," called the pastor. "Good to see you back with us. I see you brought a friend tonight." He turned his attention to Gabe. "Do you wish to introduce yourself? If not, that's okay, but it sometimes helps to break the ice."

Just introducing himself wouldn't hurt. "My name is Gabriel Pechman. Most folks call me Gabe. I've lived here for about six months now. I moved from up north—Pennsylvania."

"Pennsylvania! What a lovely state," said the pastor. "I've been there a few times. The mountains are tremendous."

Gabe nodded, praying he'd move on to another person. Thankfully, he did, and Gabe breathed a sigh of relief. He was not ready to talk about his grief to a bunch of strangers.

As if reading his thoughts, Bill whispered again, "Strangers are sometimes easier to talk to. And they're all dealing with grief too."

"But I wanted to get back into the Word, not my feelings." Gabe festered in his own anger as the pastor chatted on with some other folks. Then he readdressed the whole audience.

"This week, let's discuss another stage of grief—depression."

Several men moaned in the crowd, and Gabe couldn't agree more.

"Depression can have many stages and look different for a lot of folks," said the pastor, coming around the lectern to stand more in front of the crowd. "Depression can mean shutting yourself off from the world, not caring about your personal hygiene ... maybe you often feel foggy or confused by things. Simple things, like meeting new friends or getting back into life, seem hard, complicated. Although we know the stages of grief don't present in the same order to all people, grief depression usually signals a time when you have finally processed some things, and you might be ready to move forward." He looked around the room and asked, "Who thinks they have experienced this stage already or may be in it now."

Bill immediately raised his hand, and Gabe felt startled. His friend had been depressed? Or *is* depressed? Gabe didn't raise his hand. He wasn't sure what stage he was in. He didn't feel depressed really ... just sluggish. Like life didn't matter without Ellie.

"You should have put your hand up," Bill whispered.

"I should? You think I'm depressed?"

"Gentleman?" the pastor called. "Care to share?"

Gabe scowled at Bill, but his friend turned to the pastor, unaware.

"Yes, Pastor Tim. I was just saying I think Gabe should have raised his hand. I know I'm not supposed to push, but I've seen the signs in him, and as a friend, I'm worried."

Pastor Tim moved to stand next to Gabe and put his hand on his shoulder. "Bill, I admire your concern for your friend, but Gabe needs to go at his own pace, remember? We can't force anyone to go through these steps at our speed." He looked back around the room. "Each person experiences things in their own way and in their own time." He squeezed Gabe's shoulder and looked back down at him. "If you want to share, you can, but don't feel obligated."

Gabe shook his head slightly, and the pastor nodded with a smile.

When he moved on to another man in the group, Gabe began to assess. *Maybe I am depressed. When Ellie died, my whole world toppled over.*

Several men around the room nodded as the other man talked, but Gabe felt like they were giving him affirmation.

He thought about how he'd moved here because Ellie had wanted to live in a warmer climate. He realized how stupid that sounded. *I was a crappy husband. I waited until she was dead to fulfill her dream.* Gabe choked back a sob. Maybe he was depressed *and* angry.

What were all the stages of grief? Anger, depression … denial. He couldn't remember the others. Had he gone through them already or was he still processing. How long did it take to go through them all?

Gabe sniffled as he listened to the other man finish his story and watched as the pastor moved on with his lesson.

Bill reached out to Gabe with a handkerchief. Gabe pushed it away. "You shouldn't have done this, Bill." Gabe rose and bolted from the room, his resolve to stay and see it through dissipating like a wet drop of rain in a roaring fire.

In the parking lot, he was pacing back and forth next to their car when Bill walked up to him.

"I'll take you home. I'm sorry I pushed. But this group has helped me so much. When Phyllis died there was no one there to tell me how I would be feeling or that those feelings were normal. I—"

Gabe put a hand up to stop him. "I can't do this, Bill. I'm not ready."

Bill nodded and put his hand on Gabe's shoulder. "I get it. I see you hole yourself away from people, and I know that isn't good. Many people can't handle grief alone." His friend wiped a hand over his face. "I've seen some give into the depression, and now I'm grieving them too. I don't want that to happen to you, Gabe." Bill hiccupped a sob and pulled out his handkerchief. "I know that sounds dumb. We've only known each other a few months. Gladys says I invest in people too quickly."

Gabe swallowed the lump in his own throat. How could he be angry at someone who clearly cared about him so much.

"I didn't ask you to care." He tried to squelch the warring emotions inside his brain.

Bill was his opposite—always caring, worrying about others. Gabe had felt accepted and loved right from the start with Bill, even though he'd kept the older man at arm's length.

"Do you know that story of Moses, Aaron, and Hur?"

Gabe frowned. "I don't think so."

"Moses held up his staff while Joshua was fighting the Amalekites. When he had his staff up, they were winning. If he put it down, they would start losing. So, Aaron and Hur came to help. They put a stone down for him to sit on and then helped him hold up the staff. Joshua defeated the

Amalekites because they all worked together. That's what friends do." Bill wiped his handkerchief across his nose. "I see you struggling, and I want to help."

He knew Bill was right—he needed help. But he wasn't sure this was the way just yet.

He leaned against Bill's car and waited for the older man to pull himself together. When Bill put up a finger to explain himself further, Gabe put out his hand to stop him once more.

"No more tonight. I do forgive you, and I hear what you're saying. I need a bit more time."

## Chapter Sixteen

*One day to go.*

"We're going to go this way today, girl." Gabe turned the opposite direction from their norm, causing Daisy to pull at the leash. He pulled and she obeyed, immediately putting her nose to the ground to sniff new territory.

He'd awakened this morning almost an hour before his alarm with thoughts racing through his head from the night before. Was he depressed? Sure. His wife was dead. What normal person wouldn't feel depressed? Wasn't that the way he'd feel from now until his own death? He'd assumed this was what being a widower meant—depression, loneliness, a constant state of malaise.

As Daisy stopped to sniff at a clump of brown grass, he dug his phone from his pocket and noticed another missed call from his sister. She would be at work now, and he wasn't ready to talk. He needed to be "in the mood." And he still needed to process the things he'd heard last night. Maybe he was finally starting to make a turn for the better, but what would that mean for his life? Would he forget Ellie and the many happy years they had been together? He didn't want that. Would that mean he needed to move again? And if so, where? He couldn't imagine going back to the town where they had lived—there were some friends there—most had given up on him long ago though—but also memories.

Daisy pulled again, and he stopped to let her sniff and do her business. He noticed an open path to the beach across the road to his right. When Daisy finished, they crossed the road and walked up the trail to the beach. The way was easier here, with a smaller dune to cross. Why had he not noticed this path before?

When they crested the small dune, the empty beach lay before them. The sun was just beginning to crest the horizon. Gabe wondered if he'd ever seen a more beautiful light. Red, yellows, purples, and blues washed over the ocean in a riot of color. In another moment, the scene changed as the skies filled with a blossom of red hues. Daisy led Gabe toward the water as the sun made its entrance for the day. Gabe sat down hard in the sand, never taking his eyes off God's glory.

"Why, God? Why did you take her from me? You give so much beauty to the world. Look at that sunrise. From a star that is billions of miles away, we get this gorgeous sky. When I met Ellie, I knew you had given her to me, and I had to protect her, love her, cherish her." A sob choked him, and he swiped away a tear. "I tried, Lord. I tried. But the cancer was too strong." He put his head on his knees and wept. Daisy, sensing his pain, lay down at his side, head in his lap, as the sun moved higher into the sky.

"You're out here early."

Gabe started and looked up. Nora stood a few paces away, beach chair and bag in hand. She dropped both items at the sight of his face. He swiped a hand over his features, feeling foolish. He wondered if his eyes were red and how he'd explain himself.

Nora sat next to him and took his hand. "Thinking about Ellie?"

He'd forgotten he'd told her. He'd kept his grief to himself for so long and rarely spoke of his dead wife to others. Especially not to strangers. He nodded.

Nora looked at the rising sun and said, "I lost someone once. It was a long time ago. We were not married, but … it was still difficult." She sighed and looked down at her hands. "And there is … someone else who I might lose."

"Go on," Gabe urged. "I need a distraction."

She nodded. "My dad. He's been diagnosed with dementia." Tears welled in her eyes, but she wiped them away. "Someone once told me that grief never ends. And it's not a sign of weakness, nor a lack of faith. It's the price of love."

Gabe certainly felt weak and without faith but didn't say so. He'd failed Ellie on so many levels. "When she was first diagnosed, I played it cool. You know how men do. Tried to be strong for her. She fell apart and needed a strong something to hold onto. I cracked jokes. I acted aloof about it." He shook his head. "But instead of showing her strength, I think she thought I didn't care. She kept some of the pain from me, didn't let me into her struggle. I didn't know she was not getting better until it was too late."

Nora put her arm around Gabe's shoulders as he cried fresh tears.

"She died thinking I didn't care or didn't love her."

"I'm sure that isn't true. I've not known you long, but I can tell you're a man with a very deep heart. I'm guessing she knew you were hurting too."

Gabe shook his head. "You don't understand. The day she died …" Gabe paused as a sob choked his words once more. "The day … that day, she asked me to get something from the store ... a sweet treat, I think. I can't even remember now. But she didn't feel well and had not gotten out of bed. Which should have been my first clue, but I was so dumb ... so blind to what was happening. I thought I was doing the right thing—to go and get what she needed. I would do anything for her. Anything." He shook his head again and sobbed for a moment. Nora rubbed his back with long, smooth strokes. "When I came back—" A sob racked Gabe's chest, and he leaned into Nora.

"You don't have to say more. Just let it out." Nora's soothing voice made Gabe feel safe. She held no pretense, no preconceived notion of who he was or what he should be, only that he grieved. She let him for several minutes, perhaps longer, Gabe had lost track of time. When he finally sat up and looked ahead, the beach had filled with families and beach paraphernalia.

He started to rein in Daisy. "I guess we should go."

Nora's strong grip held him fast to the sand. "Don't run away from your grief." When Gabe frowned at her, she continued, "Isn't that what you have been doing? You ran away from home, from family, friends ... but you can't run away from grief. You can't run away from emotions. You have to process, Gabe, or you will always wallow in this pain."

He knew she was right, but he didn't feel ready to process. Ellie had always accused him of ignoring his emotions, but he'd always said he simply didn't have any. He knew that to be wrong. He'd loved her with the deepest emotions he'd ever felt. And he hurt when she hurt. He smiled when she smiled. But what if his emotions were tied to Ellie?

"Feeling emotions are a normal thing," Nora said, as if reading his mind. Her grip had loosened on his arm, but still held him fast. "Grief never ends, but it changes. It's a passage, not a place to stay. You won't get over the grief, but you can live with it in a lesser capacity. But you can't hide, and you can't run. You need to start living life again. A real life, not this made up one you think Ellie wants for you now."

Her words stung, but Gabe felt some truth in them. "So how do I move forward?"

Nora smiled a sad smile and looked back at the ocean. "Have you ever stood at the edge of the beach as the tide came in?"

Gabe nodded, unsure where she was going with this.

"If you stand in one spot, the waves keep coming, don't they? The tide is going to come in no matter what you do. Eventually it'll swallow you up. You'd drown, maybe, if you didn't move. But have you ever tried to surf the waves?" She looked at him, and he nodded again.

"Yeah. I used to love to go out a few paces and watch and wait for rollers." How long had it been since he'd felt that carefree? "I would gauge when the wave was coming, jump before it reached me, and bodysurf in."

"Go with the flow, right?" Nora turned to him and shielded her eyes with one hand from the sun.

Gabe suddenly understood her point. He'd been standing in one spot, expecting the waves—the grief—to go away, but they'd kept coming to drown him. Instead, he needed to jump into them, become one with them ... to flow.

## Chapter Seventeen

Nora suggested she make him some breakfast, so they moved back to her rental place.

As Gabe walked up the wooden steps to her door, he wondered if he should take Daisy home first.

"I think I should drop off Daisy. Your rental agreement might not allow dogs."

Nora waved him off as she unlocked the door and moved inside. "You can have dogs here. I just don't have one. And if you go home, you won't come back. Come on."

She wasn't wrong.

He kept Daisy leashed as he entered. The place smelled faintly of Nora's perfume and had the familiar beach decor he remembered from when he was a tourist.

"I think I have some eggs and bacon," Nora called as she mounted a set of stairs to the next level.

He remembered a few days prior when Bill had tried to cook eggs for him too and how he'd rejected the eggs. He didn't want to offend Nora, though, so he said only, "I prefer scrambled."

Upstairs in the main living space, a set of double glass doors looked out over the dune to the sea. He pushed open the sliding door and stepped out onto the wooden deck. A fresh swell of salty air hit him, and he felt the tension in his shoulder loosen. Daisy moved to the railing and sat, her nose in the air, sniffing the new smells. He patted her head as he sat in one of the Adirondack chairs.

"Blissful, isn't it?" Nora said from the doorway.

He nodded but said nothing, his gaze on the crashing surf.

"I have coffee too, sound good?"

"Don't drink the stuff," he said. "Got any soda?" He turned to look up at her, and she smiled.

"I do. Coming right up. Just give me a few minutes to cook everything up."

Gabe turned back to the view and thought about the last time he and Ellie had come to the beach.

"Did you see the hammock right outside our bedroom door, babe? I'm going to be in that a *lot!*" Ellie had said the first day.

He'd left her to her hammock that week for the most part. She'd needed some alone time, and so had he. Their jobs that summer had both been stressful and demanding, and they had needed that vacation. He remembered they had rarely eaten in—Ellie had needed time off from being a wife too.

He loved how they had complimented each other so well and the communication they always kept alive in their marriage. It was one of the things he missed the most now—the best friend he loved to talk to.

Ellie had known all his idiosyncrasies and had put up with them. He'd been overly obsessive compulsive when they had married. Over time, he'd learned to live with a woman and realized some of his compulsive tendencies could be scrapped. But he'd also noticed Ellie had become a bit more compulsive with some things too—they had changed each other into the best versions of themselves.

He sighed and leaned his head back against the chair. When was the last time he'd sat and enjoyed the breeze, the sun, the birds singing. He'd not even read a book in so long—something he used to love to do. Now he found his mind couldn't let him sink into a story. He always ended up thinking about Ellie and wondering if she'd like the book or not.

A swoosh sounded from behind him, and Nora said, "Breakfast is ready."

After eating and some simple small talk, Gabe rose from the table and grabbed Daisy's leash.

"I should really get back. Bill might need me at the shop." He knew Bill was not expecting him today, but he needed an excuse to get away.

"I'll walk you down."

He waved her off. He needed time to think on his own today. "No, but thanks. I really appreciate the breakfast."

"Okay."

She looked disappointed, but Gabe still felt the need to guard his heart. She'd be leaving soon, and he was not ready for any kind of relationship anyway. What was he saying? She'd been nice like a friend. He didn't even know what this was.

"Well, I hope to see you again before I leave," she said as she petted Daisy on the head.

"Maybe." He smiled and didn't commit more. Tomorrow would be a hard day for him, and he was not sure he would let himself out of the house. He offered her a small wave and walked down the steps and out the door.

## Chapter Eighteen

When he'd taken about ten steps from Nora's rental, he heard his name. He turned to see Hattie waving to him from the next house over.

"Gabriel! Come here, son." She pointed one gnarled finger to the steps leading up to her deck.

He sighed. He'd never been there before and wondered at the coincidence of her living next to his new friend.

*You don't believe in coincidence,* he heard Ellie's voice in his head.

"Hey, Hattie, what's going on."

The old woman took a moment to pet Daisy and give her kisses before saying, "I need some help inside."

She led the way into a smaller home than the rental he'd just been in. The living space on the second floor had similar sliding glass doors looking out to the beach, but the decor was less "beachy." Instead of teals, pinks, and seafoam green, Hattie's house was filled with warm dark colors like burgundy and brown. And instead of the long, wraparound couch he'd seen in Nora's place, two brown recliners sat dead center in front of the television and fireplace. Gabe noticed the deck held two Adirondack chairs. When he turned to look at the dining area, he saw a table only big enough for two chairs as well.

It was obvious Hattie didn't have many visitors and that this house had been for her and her husband alone.

Gabe wondered if Ellie would have liked something similar—a place just for them in their retirement. But no, he decided, Ellie had liked hosting friends and having people over. They would have had seating for many.

Just then a gray ball of fur streaked across the living room floor. Gabe jumped, and Daisy strained on the leash, ears on alert.

"What the …?"

"That's Sassy, my cat."

"Maybe I should have taken Daisy home first."

"Nonsense. Let her off that leash. She can fend for herself." Hattie reached down and unclasped the leash, and Daisy went flying.

"Daisy! No!"

Too late, Gabe watched as Daisy cornered the cat. As she leaned in, the cat hissed and batted Daisy's snout with a paw. With a yelp, his dog sat back and shook her head.

"See?" said Hattie. "Animals got natural instincts and defenses. They'll be friends before too long." She smiled and pointed to one of the sliding glass doors. "I'm so glad you came along. I can't get this durn door unstuck."

Gabe tried to open the door. Sure enough, it stuck.

"I don't suppose you have any WD40?"

Hattie's scrunched nose gave him his answer. "Dubba what, darlin'?"

"Like a lubricant kind of thing for metal."

"Can't say as I do." She turned to look into the kitchen then back at him. "How 'bout cookin' spray?"

"That might work."

Hattie toddled into the kitchen, Daisy trailing behind her. Apparently, the cat had been forgotten for now. Hattie turned to her. "Sit."

Daisy obliged, looking lovingly up at the old woman, her tail thumping out a rhythm. But when Hattie turned to go to the kitchen again, Daisy trailed behind.

"Well, land's sakes, dog. I told you to sit."

"But you didn't say stay," Gabe called.

Hattie came back into the room with the spray, Daisy still following. "Here you go."

Gabe sprayed the door jamb and waited a few moments before trying to open the door again. With a little muscle, it slowly opened. He sprayed some more oil into other parts of the door and then opened and closed it several times to lubricate it fully. He opened the door fully and stepped out to the deck. Inspecting the door frame, he sprayed a bit more. Before heading inside, he glanced over at Nora's rental and noticed the pool. Perhaps he should tell her about Hattie's proclivity for spying.

He moved back into the house and handed Hattie back the cooking spray. "There you go. That should work for a bit."

"Oh, what a handy little thing. Who knew this was for more than just cooking?" She laughed. "Now I can keep to watching my neighbors." She gave him a wink. "I saw you out there on the deck next door. Didn't know you knew anyone over here."

This old lady didn't miss a thing, he thought. Even with a stuck door. "Her name's Nora. She's a tourist. I met her the other day on the beach, then in the coffee shop. And at the store."

"Land's sakes. Seems like you're meant to know one another." She patted Gabe on the shoulder and walked toward the little table. "Come sit a spell and tell me about it."

"I really should get going, Hattie. Bill might need me at the shop." He'd given Nora this same lie—no need to start too many lies today. And Daisy was starting to investigate the cornered cat once more.

"Nonsense." Hattie waved an arthritic hand over her shoulder. "I know you took the day off. I was down there earlier. Bill was puffing away on one of those damnable cancer sticks when I popped in. I gave him what for about it." She pulled a Diet Coke from the fridge and sat it down at one of the table chairs.

He told Daisy to be good and turned back to Hattie. "You like Diet Coke too?"

"Gracious no. Stuff will rot your teeth and cause dementia. But Bill told me you liked it, so I bought a few in case you ever happened by." She pulled a mug from the cupboard and filled it with some hot water before popping it into the microwave to heat.

"You bought Diet Coke for me for if I ever just *happened* to stop by?" Gabe couldn't understand this older woman. He'd lived here six months and had not even known where she lived until now. Another coincidence?

A shiver ran up his spine as he sat at the table and popped open the soda.

When the microwave beeped, Hattie removed the mug and dunked a tea bag and some sugar in. She stirred the tea as she shuffled to the table.

Another hiss emitted from the corner and another yelp. Gabe called for Daisy to let the poor cat alone, and she mostly complied—retreating a few feet away and staring into the corner.

"Momma taught me to be prepared is all. And after running into you the other day on my walk, I had a feeling you would get here soon enough." Hattie looked up from her tea and said, "Is it today?"

"Is what today?" Gabe took a sip of his soda.

"Anniversary of some sort. Birthday. Day you met. Something bringing you down or causing some sorrow. I could see it in your eyes the other day and the last few times I saw you. Some big day of grief was coming. I'd seen it before in my own eyes." She sipped at her tea and squinted at him. Then, eyes lighting up, she stood abruptly and shuffled again to the kitchen cupboards. "I have Lorna Doones!"

Gabe wanted to chuckle, but her insight had rattled him.

His phone pinged, momentarily distracting his thoughts, but he didn't check it. Probably his sister again. He really needed to call her soon.

Hattie returned to the table and held out a tin full of the shortbread cookies.

He shook his head, and she sat down. "So? What is it?" She dipped a cookie into her tea and then pulled it out and bit off a small bite.

"Anniversary," said Gabe. "Of my wife's death. It's tomorrow."

Hattie dropped the cookie onto the table and grabbed Gabe's hand. He contemplated the crumbs that had fallen from the cookie onto the table. His life had been about as dry and unstable as that cookie this past year. Everyone had said the first year was the hardest—birthdays, anniversaries, holidays. They had not been joking, but he'd been counting down to this date as if everything would change after it. He longed to get back to a normal life where grief didn't play such a huge factor.

His phone rang, but he ignored it again without looking at it. His sister was getting persistent. She knew the date was tomorrow too and probably worried as well. He would definitely call her later.

He looked back at Hattie, who had remained unusually quiet while he worked through his thoughts.

"Oh, darlin', that's a big one," she said. "What do you plan to do to pass the time? I hope you're working or spending some time with friends."

Gabe had left all his friends behind. All he wanted to do tomorrow was lie in bed and wallow in his grief.

"You must not wallow." He looked up, startled. How was it that everyone seemed to be able to read his thoughts lately? "I know that's what I wanted to do that first-year anniversary. But you must not." She waggled her finger at him, her bangles jingling. "You'll come here, or we'll go out. You plan. We could take a trip up north. Or spend time on the beach, or—"

He pulled his hand away from hers and shook his head. "No, Hattie. Just ... no." He rose then. "I really should get back to ... well, I want to be alone."

He knew he'd promised Bill and Gladys dinner at their house tonight, but the day had already been too much. He'd call them and cancel. It would disappoint Bill for sure, but eventually he would forgive him.

Hattie rose too, just as Gabe's phone rang again. "Seriously, Sis, I'll call later!" He pulled the phone from his pocket and noticed the number was not his sister's but Bill's.

"Bill, what's up?" Gabe felt the panic rise in his chest. Bill rarely called him—he could simply come upstairs and chat when he needed. Maybe it was about dinner.

"No, Gabe, it's Gladys."

It sounded like she was crying. "Gladys, what's wrong? Where's Bill?"

"Please come quick. Bill's had …" Gabe heard her choke back a sob. "Bill's had a heart attack."

## Chapter Nineteen

Gabe's truck tires squealed as he pulled into the parking lot of the Outer Banks Hospital. The truck had barely been run since he'd moved to Avon and had given him a bit of trouble starting. And that was after he'd rummaged his apartment for the keys. Putting the truck in park, he leapt from the vehicle and rushed through the main entrance doors of the hospital, fearing he'd be too late. Almost an hour had passed on the drive to Nags Head since Gladys' phone call. What if he never saw Bill again?

He stopped at the information desk and inquired about his friend.

"I'm looking for William Brower. He was brought in with a heart attack."

"He'd probably still be in the ER," the older woman behind the counter said. Her pink vest felt too festive and bright for Gabe. "Let me check."

Her nails tapped on her keyboard a minute, and she squinted at the screen. She rummaged around at her desk, and Gabe felt like screaming for her to hurry. Finding her glasses, she put them on and looked again at her computer screen.

"That's better. Now ... let's see."

Gabe felt his tension building to a boiling point. He looked down the hall. Maybe he'd try to find the ER first. How big could this—

"Ah, here it is. Yes. He's in the ER right now." She looked down the hallway and pointed with one gnarled finger. "Down this hall, take a right, and then a left. You can't miss it."

Gabe had started down the hallway before she'd even finished her instructions.

"Don't run!" she called behind him.

*Yeah, right, lady.*

He waited until she was out of sight and then put his body into fourth gear. His sneakers slapped the linoleum as he sped through the halls, narrowly missing several nursing staff as he rounded the last corner. Briefly, as he struggled for breath, he chided himself for not keeping up his running routine.

There, sitting among other patients waiting to be seen, sat Gladys. She put a tissue up to her nose as she looked around. Spotting Gabe, she came to her feet and held out her hands. He rushed to her and put his arm around her shoulders.

"Here, sit back down. What's going on with Bill?"

Gladys sat down and wiped her nose once more. "The doctors are in there now, but I can't be. Why can't I be?" She looked at Gabe with glistening eyes. "I'm his wife!" She yelled the last toward the poor nurse behind the desk.

Gabe patted her hand and shot the nurse an apologetic glance. "Gladys, they have to check him out without interference. I'm sure they'll be out soon. Tell me what happened."

Gladys sighed. "I had come into the shop with some baked goods, like I do every day. But Bill was not around—

or at least I didn't see him. When I walked around the count—" She broke into a sob and Gabe pulled her close. "He ... he was lying on the floor. Oh, Gabe, he looked so pale. I called the ambulance right away, but you know it takes forever here. It felt like an eternity until they came."

"Was he awake at all during that time?"

Gladys nodded. "Some. He was in and out. That's how I knew it was a heart attack. He kept saying he couldn't breathe, and his chest hurt. That's what happened to my Charlie too." She bit back another sob before falling against Gabe's shoulder.

If only Gabe had gone to work today. If only he'd checked in. What kind of friend was he? In fact, he'd been thinking about canceling dinner with them. Bill and Gladys had done so much for him—had tried to do so much. And yet he'd only been thinking about himself again. When would he change his ways and start thinking of others? He hit his leg with his fist.

*Lord, please help Bill. Please, Lord. I'll do better. I want to do better. I want to care for these folks the way they care for me.*

Just then the nurse at the front desk came over to them. Blonde and petite, she looked young and vital. Gabe remembered when he'd felt vital once.

"Mrs. Brower?" When Gladys nodded, the nurse said, "Would you come with me, please?"

Gladys stood and grabbed Gabe's hand. "This is our son, can he come too?"

Gabe's heart swelled at her title for him. Perhaps she simply wanted someone to come with her and knew that would be the only way. Gabe secretly hoped she meant the title, though, because he suddenly realized Bill felt like a dad to him.

"Certainly. Right this way."

As they followed the nurse, the typical hospital smell came to Gabe, and he pushed aside the emotions that came with that odor. He couldn't think of Ellie now. Gladys and Bill needed him to be strong, to be stable.

The nurse led them to a small office and asked them to sit. "The doctor will be here in a moment to talk with you."

Gladys held out a hand to stop the nurse. "When can I see Bill? Is he okay? Please tell me."

The nurse squatted next to Gladys and took her hand. "Your husband is currently stable, but we've lots of stuff to hook up and vitals to take right now. I promise we're taking the best care of Mr. Brower, and you'll hopefully be able to see him soon." She glanced up at Gabe and then turned back to Gladys. "My name is Erin. I'm the head nurse on staff today. If you need anything, please come find me. The doctor will be in very soon." She patted the older woman's hand and stood.

When the nurse had left the small office, Gladys began wringing her hands. Gabe put his over hers and squeezed. "I'm here. It's going to be okay."

Gabe had spent far too much time in hospitals for his young life. Ellie's mom had been terminally ill when they met, then her father had open heart surgery and eventually died of a heart attack. And then Ellie ...

He shook his mind of the memories. He needed to focus on Gladys now.

The door opened, and a doctor with salt and pepper hair and beard walked through. He held out his hand. "Hello. I'm Dr. Chiron. I'm the on-call cardiologist." He shook both their hands and sat opposite Gladys but looked at Gabe. "Your relationship to the Browers is ...?"

Gabe turned to Gladys, who said, "He's our son."

Dr. Chiron frowned but let the lie slide. Gabe was sure Bill's files couldn't have mentioned him, but he hoped the doctor would accept it and move on.

The doctor looked at a handheld computer and said to Gladys, "Mr. Brower—your husband—has had a significant cardiac event." He looked up over the top of his wire-framed glasses. "A heart attack. A pretty big one."

"You don't have to dumb it down for me, doctor. I'm not an idiot."

Gabe put his arm around her shoulders and pulled himself closer. "It's okay, Gl—Mom. Just let him talk."

Dr. Chiron frowned again but continued. "He's currently sleeping, which is good. We're monitoring his vitals. Often, these types of heart attacks can have subsequent attacks, and we want to ensure we can react in a timely manner. Once we have your husband completely stable, we'll want to do a percutaneous coronary intervention which should show us where any blockages are. Once we're able to locate those, we can treat them, probably by inserting a stent."

"How soon can you do that, and what is the risk to him?" Gabe asked, being careful to use pronouns instead of names, lest he slip up.

Dr. Chiron consulted his screen again. "We can probably do the surgery within the hour. The risk to Mr. Brower is similar to other surgeries. He could have another heart attack while we're in there. Does he have a history of heart attacks or any other issues?"

Gladys shook her head. "He's on blood pressure medication. But he's never had a heart attack that I'm aware of."

The doctor nodded. "Yes, I see we've noted the medication here." He looked up and offered his first smile. "Mrs. Brower, this is a common course to take after a heart attack. Please know we take your husband's health and well-being very seriously. *I* take it seriously." He looked at Gabe. "Do you have kids? Grandkids for these two?"

Gabe swallowed hard but shook his head. He hated lying—he'd never been very good at it.

"Well ... do you have any other questions?"

"Can I see him?"

"Yes, of course." The doctor rose and Gladys with him. "Follow me."

The trio walked from the room and down a short hallway and through a set of double doors. On the other side, the emergency room thrummed with activity. As the doctor guided them down the hallway, a shrill beeping began, and a team of nurses pushed past them with a cart.

Dr. Chiron stopped and turned to Gladys and Gabe. "You'll have to go back to the waiting room now. I'm sorry. We'll come get you when we've stabilized him again." He gently took Gladys's arm and turned her, indicating for Gabe to follow. Nurse Erin came from behind a desk, and the doctor instructed her to guide them out. Then he turned and ran for the room.

Gladys's knees buckled, and Gabe had to grab her underneath her armpits. "No! I want to see my husband!"

"Ma'am, please just let them do their jobs. We'll come get you as soon as possible."

Gabe and Nurse Erin practically dragged Gladys down the short hallway and back out into the waiting room. Those waiting their turn stared at the old lady on the verge of a mental breakdown. Gladys had collapsed into sobs and refused to walk. Gabe finally led her to a chair, and the nurse brought her a plastic cup of water.

"Here, Mrs. Brower. Please try to calm down. Your husband is being attended to by the best we have right now." She looked up at Gabe. "I'm going to go back in. Are you okay with her?"

He nodded but felt his heart plummet as she walked away. He turned back to Gladys, who was wailing and causing a scene.

"Gladys. Stop. Please." When Gladys refused, he grabbed her hand and began to pray. "Lord, we need you right now. Gladys needs you. Bill needs you. Those doctors and nurses need you. Please don't take Bill from us."

Gabe noticed Gladys had calmed down and was watching him now with interest. He said a hasty amen, and the silence between them grew.

"I didn't think you prayed ... or even knew God," Gladys said.

Had he seemed like that much of a heathen? Even when he'd not been overly boisterous about his faith, he'd been told others could see it within him. Had he let his relationship with God slip so far?

He cleared his throat. "I'm a Christian. I haven't been on speaking terms with God in a while." His mouth cocked into a smirk. "Not sure he'll listen to me at this point, so you might want to do some praying of your own."

Gladys dug a wadded-up tissue from her pocket and wiped at her nose. "He listens more than you think."

Gabe found a tissue box sitting on a nearby table and brought it to her. "I'm not so sure."

"'Behold, I'm with you always'," Gladys quoted.

Gabe leaned in and whispered, "'Be strong and courageous. Don't be frightened, and don't be dismayed, for the Lord your God is with you wherever you go.' If you know your Bible, you should know that one too. If God is here, he is here for you and Bill too. To quote a non-Christian singer, 'You gotta have faith'."

Gladys scowled at him, but then her face fell slack. "I know. But what will I do without Bill?"

Gabe offered a little chuckle. "You're asking the wrong person."

Her look of surprise and regret indicated Gladys had not thought before she'd spoke. "Oh Gabe, I'm sorry. How heartless—"

Gabe held up a hand to stop her. "Let it go. Gee, I'm quoting all sorts of songs today." He tried to smile, but her concerned look continued. "We'll get through this together, how about that?" He grabbed her hand and squeezed. "All three of us."

## Chapter Twenty

Gabe woke with a kink in his neck. Gladys had wanted to stay at the hospital, and the staff had managed a bed for her in Bill's room, but Gabe had spent the night in a waiting room chair. As he sat up straighter, he thought of the phone call he'd made to Hattie last night. After Gladys had called to tell him about Bill, Hattie had agreed to watch Daisy until he returned. He'd checked in late last night to see if it was okay if he stayed at the hospital. He couldn't justify driving the hour back to Avon if Gladys needed him here.

"Of course, dear. This pup ain't no bother. Her and Sassy are gettin' along just fine. I fed her some hamburger. Hope that's okay."

"She'll love you forever, and I'll probably never get her to eat kibble again." He worried about Daisy's delicate stomach but felt thankful for this new friend. After telling Hattie he'd call in the morning, they had hung up.

He rose and stretched, wishing the waiting room had big windows like his hospital back home. He never realized how encouraging it was to see the sun. Taking a deep breath, he moved toward the doors. He needed some of that fresh air.

"Mr. Brower?"

He turned and saw Nurse Erin coming toward him. "No, I'm—" and then he remembered. He was their son. His last name would be Brower. He smiled instead and kept his mouth shut.

"Mrs. Brower was concerned about you and had me get you this." She held out a plastic cup with a lid and straw. "Diet, right?"

Gabe smiled and accepted the cup. "Thank you. I can really use this." He took a sip and sighed. "I was going to get some fresh air. Is everything okay?"

A look of unease passed across the nurse's face that Gabe couldn't decipher. "He's currently stable. They're pretty sure he needs open heart surgery, but they would like to do more tests. Open heart surgery is a big deal, and they don't want to go in if they don't have to."

Gabe let this information sink in while he took another sip and looked again at the door. The news made sense, but the fear of the unknown prickled at his skin.

"You've been here since last night? That's a long shift."

Nurse Erin nodded. "A double. I'll be getting off my shift soon, though, but I wanted to give you that update. I hope your dad is going to be okay. Dr. Chiron is one of the best. And I hope you get some rest soon. I know that chair couldn't have been easy to sleep in."

"Thanks. It certainly was not, but I guess I'll sleep better tonight. I hope you can get some rest too."

She laughed. "With two small kids who are just now rising and shining ... and bouncing all over the place? Not likely. But they'll take naps later."

He smiled as she walked away with a wave. He turned and left the building for the first time in almost fourteen hours.

The salty air filled his nostrils almost immediately, and he breathed in deeply. How he loved that smell and the way his allergies had stayed at bay since living here. He checked his phone to see several missed calls again from his sister. It would be too early to ring her now, but he would definitely call today.

Today. Today was the day. Surprised he'd not thought of it first thing, he took another sip of his soda and let his mind wander.

He thought of the last time he'd been in a hospital—a little over a year ago. He'd been the one with the extra bed that time. Ellie beside him in the uncomfortable hospital bed, he'd longed to crawl up next to her and hold her close. He remembered the beeping of the machines and the way the place smelled—antiseptic and sadness. Ellie had looked as pale as the sheets, her hair a riotous mess from tossing and turning in pain. His hand clutched hers while she slept. Even when he slept, which was not much.

She'd not wanted to be in the hospital at the end, and they had moved back to the house against the doctor's suggestion. But the hospital had packed them up with gear and medication when he'd taken her home—a decision he regretted to this day. If only they had stayed in the hospital, where doctors and nurses who knew more could have helped ... perhaps Ellie would still be alive.

But he knew that to not be true. She'd have held on just to go home, and that would have been unfair to her. When Ellie wanted certain things, she fought for them. Being home in her own bed would have been something she'd have fought for until the end. And she did. But then he'd failed at keeping her alive.

After drinking the rest of the soda, Gabe dropped the cup into a trash can.

He'd thought about moving back to Iowa—where he'd grown up—before moving here. He shuddered. Iowa. Why would anyone want to move there? His parents had made a life there, but he couldn't imagine doing the same.

The Outer Banks was definitely better than Iowa. And now he felt like he had some friends he didn't want to leave. Couldn't leave if Bill needed him. Gabe knew he needed to start doing things differently if he stayed. He couldn't keep living this life that wasn't his own. Instead of living a life Ellie would want, he needed to live a life she'd want for him.

"When I die, you better not become a hermit," she'd told him. "That's why you need to find a hobby or something you enjoy."

"I enjoy being with you. And we'll be together a long time, so when you die, I'll just lie down and die too," he'd told her.

He'd envisioned them both old, decrepit, and in failing health. He never envisioned Ellie dead before the age of fifty-five.

He groaned and let the tears come. He sank onto a bench and put his head into his hands. Crying had not come easy to him. He'd always put a stopper in it except when alone, at night, drunk. Now the tears came easily as he considered all he'd lost and still had the potential of losing. He'd lost the love of his life, had abandoned his only family, moved to a place he was not sure he should have, and met and ignored new friends who had tried very hard to make him feel welcome. What was wrong with him?

When the tears had abated, he sat up straight and wiped the wetness from his cheeks. He'd been such a failure, but he wanted to do better. He'd bring Bill and Gladys into his life, treat them as family, and talk with his sister more often. It was time to get out of this funk.

*Changing Tides*

First things first, though. He walked back into the hospital in search of Gladys.

## Chapter Twenty-One

Two hours later, Gabe pulled into the parking lot behind the coffee shop. Gladys' pastor had come to the hospital with his wife, telling Gabe he could go home and get some real rest. They would call when they knew more. As he turned off the ignition to his truck, he noticed a car with Virginia plates.

*What's my sister doing here?*

He was barely out of the car before his sister came barreling down the outside steps from his apartment. "Oh, thank God. I've been so worried. Where were you? I've been trying to call you for hours!"

"Cameron, what are you doing here?" He looked up at his open apartment door. "And how did you get into my apartment?"

"When I got here, the shop was closed so I started banging on your door. I had driven all night … well, I left around midnight when I couldn't get ahold of you." She pulled him into a quick hug, but just as quickly let go. "I wondered why I didn't hear Daisy, so I forced open a window and shimmied inside. Then the cops came." She laughed. "I guess the neighbors thought I was breaking in or—"

"You *did* break in."

Cameron stuck her hand on her hip. "Right, but you left the window unlocked so it's not really *breaking* and entering. I showed them some pictures you had of us together—thanks for keeping those by the way. I see you don't have many others in the house." She gave him a look of disdain which he chose to ignore. "They decided I could stay, but the neighbors have been checking in on me. And an older woman—Hattie, I think—came and told me where you were."

Daisy came bounding down the steps then, her feet barely making contact with the steps. She leaped for Gabe, and he had to brace himself to keep from falling.

"Hattie left her with me," Cameron told him. "After I gave proof of ID." She rolled her eyes.

Thank God for Hattie. He would have to take her up sometime on that beer and poolside chat. He felt bad now about running out on her but knew she'd understand.

"Why don't you ever answer my calls?" Cameron frowned at him.

He knelt to pet Daisy who had brought her purple rhino toy with her. "You know this doesn't leave the house, girl." He stood and motioned to his sister. "Let's go back inside."

"I was so worried when you didn't answer any of my calls or texts," she said as she trailed him inside.

"I know." Daisy rushed past them both to get back into the house. *That dog has only one speed.* But Gabe wanted to get back inside too. Who knew what other neighbors were lurking about listening.

When they reentered the apartment, he went first to the fridge for a soda. What he really wanted was a beer, but it was only ten in the morning and his sister, despite her own affinity for alcohol, might frown upon his choice. He didn't need to give her any more ammunition to stay.

"I didn't want you to be alone today." She sat down on the couch, and Daisy followed suit, pushing herself onto Cameron's lap for attention.

"I'm not alone. I have friends here." Friends he just discovered, it seemed. Up until a few days ago, he'd felt very alone in this place. But now his connection to Gladys, Bill, and even Hattie felt like a lifeline.

"Oh," his sister said, frowning. "That's good, I guess. How's your friend? Bill, right?"

Gabe swallowed a gulp of soda, then said, "Not great. He had a heart attack. They're doing some kind of procedure this morning, but Gladys told me to get back for Daisy. And her pastor is there now with his wife."

"I did feed her a bit of kibble." Cameron petted Daisy's head and the pup rolled over for belly rubs. "She seemed hungry, and I wasn't sure how long you'd been gone or if Hattie had fed her." She scowled at him. "I'd know these things if you'd answer your phone."

"Okay. I get it. I'll be better. And thanks." He sat down on the couch and Daisy abandoned his sister for his lap. "I'm sorry, girl. But you would have done the same." He nuzzled her neck, and she dropped her toy to lick his face.

Cameron shifted on the couch to look at him. "Are you okay?"

He shrugged. "I haven't been." At her widened eyes, he quickly added, "Not to that extent. Just not really living life. But then things started happening—"

Cameron sat back against the couch and crossed her arms. "I really want you to consider moving back with me. I'm worried about you. I noticed you hadn't even unpacked yet. You've been here six months."

"I unpacked. Just ... not everything." He really needed to get to those boxes, but working two jobs and ... well, running from his grief, had been exhausting. He took another sip of his soda.

"You could move back to Maryland," Cameron said, sitting now on the edge of the couch. "At least you'd be closer, and we could see each other more."

"You could check up on me more," Gabe said.

"Well ... yes. After last December when you ..."

"I won't do that again." Gabe touched her knee. "I promise."

When she nodded that she understood, he sat back in his chair.

"But I don't think I want to move back. Or ... at least not yet. I need to see how things play out here. Gladys and Bill need me now."

A knock sounded on his door, and Daisy leapt from the couch to bark. Gabe rose and answered the door, surprised to see Nora standing on his porch.

"Uh ... hi." She offered a little wave. "I saw your truck was back ... uh, when I came this morning to get some coffee, a neighbor told me what happened. And—Oh!" Nora said as she noticed Gabe's sister sitting on the couch. "I didn't realize you had company. I can come back later or ... well, I'm leaving tomorrow so ... oh, I'm rambling. Sorry. I'll go."

Gabe reached out and grabbed her elbow as she turned to go. "Stop. It's okay. Come in." He pulled her arm slightly, and she grinned. He stepped back as she entered, corralled Daisy into the house, and shut the door. "Nora, this is my sister, Cameron. Sis, this is Nora. She's here for the week and has become a regular customer downstairs." He smiled, and Nora smiled back as she held out her hand.

"Nice to meet you."

Cameron rose from the couch and shook hands, a bewildered look on her face.

"Your brother is a great guy. It's been delightful getting to know him this week."

His sister seemed at a loss for words, so he jumped in.

"Nora met Daisy first. I was just the guy at the other end of the leash. And she likes Bill's coffee."

Nora turned to him then and asked, "How is Bill?"

As he filled Nora in on Bill's condition and possible procedures, they moved back to sit in the living room—the women, including Daisy, on the couch and he in his recliner. Soon the ladies were chatting about their lives, Gabe mostly forgotten. Although Cameron mentioned how Gabe was going to move back with her about every other sentence. Nora glanced at him, and he offered a small shake of his head. It felt good to have people in his home, people who cared. But he wasn't moving back with his sister. At least, not yet. He thought briefly about offering food or drink but wasn't sure he had anything left in the fridge.

He rose to check. "I'll be right back."

In the kitchen, he found some crackers in the cupboard and a still viable block of cheese in the fridge. He rummaged through his cupboards for something nice to set the snack on and came across a blue glass dish that Ellie had loved. He fought back the ping of grief as he plated the food. But he couldn't hold it back. Not today.

Before he knew it, he'd collapsed on the floor, sobbing.

Warm, soft hands touched his shoulder as he cried.

"It's okay, Gabe. Let it out." His sister was a good comforter. Always had been. Probably the years of therapy she'd taken for her own issues.

Why had he moved away from his support system? He'd not realized how much he missed her until now. He'd avoided even her. Blocked the one person left who truly knew him from his life. Another wave of grief washed over him as he considered all he'd lost—things both out of his control and within.

"This is why you should move back with me," his sister said softly, rubbing his shoulder.

*Well, she had tried to be comforting for a while.*

Daisy too wanted in on the comforting and pushed her way into his lap once more. He sank his nose into her neck and sobbed some more while she tried to lick his face. Finally, she gave up and leaned against him, which made him sob more. His sister's hand on his shoulder rubbed a soothing pattern.

Soon, his tears ebbed, and he rose from the floor with his sister's aid.

"I'm sorry. Something set me off." He swiped at his wet cheeks, feeling embarrassed.

"It's really okay." His sister pulled him into a hug, and he noticed Nora watching from the doorway. She clutched her hands in front of her and looked away from their familial embrace.

"Sorry to you too, Nora," he said. She probably thought he was a mess and wondered what she was getting herself into. Well, he *was* a mess. And what was *she* here for?

Nora offered a small smile and shrugged. "You know the weird thing about grief? It surprises us. We can be feeling really fine one minute and something sets us off. And then it returns with a vengeance, right?"

He nodded and pointed to the serving tray. "It was the plate. Ellie had loved that one. I forgot I even had it until I needed something for the snacks." He choked back another sob, but then shook his head. "Sorry." His sister put an arm around his waist and led him out of the kitchen.

"Yeah. Sometimes it's the smallest trigger." Nora turned and walked back into the living room, and they followed. "I heard a laugh once that sounded like my mom's, and I broke down in the middle of a shopping mall. Can you imagine?" She laughed as she sat once more on the couch.

"Every time I drive by this one ice cream place, I think of a boyfriend who really dumped me hard," his sister confessed.

"Adam? But you're married to Paul now."

She shrugged. "That doesn't change the trauma I experienced with Adam. I don't love him anymore, but there is residual stuff there. You'd know this if you'd go to therapy like I recommended." She nudged his shoulder. "I can recommend one if you move back to DC with me."

He sighed, then frowned at his sister. "Can we talk about that moving back stuff later?"

She nodded, then moved to the corner of the couch.

He knew Ellie had had similar issues with the boyfriend—fiancé—she'd had before him. The guy had blindsided her, dumping her right before their wedding. She held onto things he'd said to her for many years—sometimes assigning the blame to Gabe. It had taken many years to build trust between him and Ellie.

His sister was right. Maybe he needed something ... someone to help him through this. But moving back with his sister was not it—he knew that much. He thought of the grief group Bill had taken him to. Maybe it was a place to start.

"I had to sell the house and move because I saw her around every corner." He thought about the time he'd come into the house from shoveling snow and could have sworn he smelled Ellie's favorite candle burning. He'd even called out to her before catching himself. Those moments felt like moving back in time abruptly. When you realize what you have done, the grief comes back even harder.

"Anyway." Nora rose once more and moved to the door. "I wanted to come and say goodbye. I'm leaving early tomorrow. I do hope Bill will be okay."

Gabe walked her to the door and motioned to his sister that he'd be right back.

Outside on the porch, Gabe leaned over the rail and said, "It was nice getting to know you. I hope you had a nice vacation."

"I did," she said as she leaned next to him. "And now I'm thinking you had a pretty good idea here. Move to the beach and forget your problems. It's much better than PA."

"You live in Pennsylvania? That's where I moved from."

"You're kidding?" She smiled. "I'm from around Pittsburgh."

Gabe shook his head. "Other side of the state, but still ... small world."

Nora nodded, then smiled.

He frowned. "But don't move to run away like I did. The problems follow. Grief follows. Remember the waves and the drowning?" He turned to look at her and their faces were close enough he could smell toothpaste on her breath.

She leaned in a bit before standing up straight. "You're right. I loved getting away and experiencing something different and being by myself, but I miss my friends and family. I especially miss my dad."

Gabe cleared his throat. Would he have kissed her if she'd leaned into it? He wasn't sure. But somehow he knew this was not the time or the woman. His heart still ached for Ellie, and he needed to deal with that better first.

And he missed his sister too, but now he had friends here. He felt torn, unsure of what steps to take next. And very aware of his sister probably watching from inside.

*Changing Tides*

He held out his hand. "Well, good luck to you. I'm glad to have made your acquaintance."

Nora laughed and slapped his hand away. "We might not be ready for kisses, but we're ready for hugs." She put her arms around his waist and pulled him close. He closed his eyes as he felt the warmth of the embrace. It felt good to let others in. He needed to do more of it.

They exchanged numbers—Nora said just so he could keep her up to date about Bill—and then said goodbye. After he watched her walk away, Gabe wondered if they would become friends. Would they be more? He doubted it. Ellie had been the only one for him. He preferred to be alone now—at least without a wife or girlfriend. But he was slowly coming to the realization that friends and family were something he couldn't live without.

He went back inside and chatted with his sister, catching up on her life and having a few more crying sessions. And avoiding more talk about moving back. But something poked at Gabe's heart. He really wanted to be at the hospital with Gladys. Or to be doing something constructive.

"Sis, I really need to go be with my friend. Can you stay and help me with Daisy?"

"Sure. I can stay a few days. But let me know what's going on." She put a finger in his face and frowned.

He agreed and grabbed his keys.

But first, he needed to stop at Hattie's.

## Chapter Twenty-Two

Hattie answered her door with little Sassy in hand. "Gabriel! I'm so glad to see you." She pulled him in for a hug. "How are Bill and Gladys? How is Daisy? That was your sister, I hope. I'd never forgive myself if I handed that beautiful pup off to a stranger, but Daisy girl seemed to know her. Oh, look at my manners. Come upstairs." She pulled the door open wider and ushered him inside. "You look like you need to sit a spell. I was just fixin' to have lunch and you can join me."

Gabe did feel like he needed to rest, but there was so much to do. He had to keep going for his friends. His stomach growled at that moment. "I could use a bite."

"Today's the day, right?" Hattie said as she led the way to the couch.

Gabe shrugged then sat. "That's not important right now. You said once we could chat about our grief. Can we do that now?"

Hattie sat down beside him with the cat on her lap. "Of course. What's on your mind, sugar?"

Gabe stroked the cat's head, and she leaned into his hand. In another moment, the feline was sitting in his lap, purring. She nestled against his stomach as he ran his hand over her back and tail. "I've missed having a cat," he said.

"So get one. There's an animal shelter right here in Avon."

"Not sure Daisy would like that."

"Pfft." Hattie waved a hand. "She'll deal. They were practically sisters by the time she left this morning."

Gabe was not so sure about that, but he could try. The need to fulfill some of his own wants and dreams felt strong. In the last year, he'd lived his life for Ellie, but the grief never lessened. Maybe this was not the way. Maybe it would be okay to do some things he wanted to do.

"How did you get over your husband's death?"

"Easy," Hattie said as she pushed herself off the couch then walked toward the kitchen. "I didn't."

Gabe had been afraid of this answer. The grief took hold even on the good days here, dragging him into an abyss he thought maybe someday he'd not be able to emerge from.

Hattie returned with a soda and two sandwiches on a plate. She held out the plate for him to snag a sandwich—shrimp salad on rye—then sat the soda next to him on the table. "But friends make it easier. Living life makes it easier. 'To every thing there is a season,' the Bible says. 'A time to live and a time to die.' Don't you believe that?" She settled back on the couch next to him and took a bite of the other sandwich.

Gabe nodded as he took another bite. "This is good," he said.

"Child, don't speak with your mouth full. Didn't your mother teach you anything?" She smirked then, and he began to see Hattie Mae Winston was not such a grump after all, but a bit of a jokester.

He swallowed then said, "Yes, ma'am." At her wink, he continued. "I do know what you're saying. We all die. It's life's cycle. I just didn't think Ellie's life cycle would be so short. I thought we had so much more time. So many more days to live, love, and do the things she wanted to do." He swallowed the lump in his throat as he finished his sandwich and then continued to give attention to Sassy. The cat turned over now, inviting him to rub the belly. Too late, he remembered the claws.

"Oh, you stupid cat." Hattie swiped her from Gabe and tossed her to the floor. Sassy shook off the reprimand and slunk away to the nearby scratching post.

"It's okay. I had cats growing up. They always want you to rub their belly but then feel prone to attack, I guess."

"Just like humans," Hattie said, taking the last bite of her sandwich.

Gabe turned to her with a frown. "What do you mean?"

Hattie put the empty plate on the table and rubbed her knee. "Durn thing's been acting up, ya know? Winter's on its way, I suspect."

Gabe looked out the double sliding doors to the blue sky and crystal-clear waters of the ocean. He couldn't imagine what winter was like here. Certainly not as cold as Pennsylvania winters. But he would miss the snow—not the shoveling, but the look.

He turned back to Hattie, awaiting her answer to his question.

"I mean that humans want attention ... love, affection ... all that too. But sometimes because we've been hurt before, we can only go so far before our protective measures kick in. And then we scratch. Or run away." She eyed him, and he could see the twinkle there of an unspoken lesson. "You gotta stop running away, sugar, and let others love on ya, even if it might hurt."

*Okay, maybe the lesson wasn't so unspoken.*

He leaned back against the sofa cushion and sighed. "I know. It's almost like I can't even avoid it like I want to. Bill and Gladys"—he looked at her—"and even you have been so great to me. And yet I kept blocking you all out. You know I've never been to Bill's house? He's invited me, like, every day practically. But I've refused every time. Made excuses." Gabe ran a hand over his face. He felt so tired. Not just from the sleepless night in the hospital chair, but from life. He looked at the bottle of soda Hattie had brought him. "Do you have any tea?"

She stared at him a moment but then stood slowly, hands on knees and pushing herself up as if she'd grown attached to the spot. "Sure. Full test or the weak stuff? I have herbal, if you're feeling particularly pathetic."

"Let's not get crazy." He laughed. "The strongest regular tea you have."

"English Breakfast it is." She shuffled off to the kitchen.

English Breakfast had been one of Ellie's favorites too. He wondered for a minute if he subconsciously had wanted the tea for her or for himself. Maybe he'd lived too long for her, and he'd not be able to find himself anymore. He looked again at the soda. No. He truly wanted the tea today—for whatever reason.

Hattie returned with a mug that said "Sarcasm: Just Another Service I Offer." He laughed then dunked the tea bag up and down. Steam rose from the mug, and he held it close to his face. Ellie had joked in the past about tea being medicinal in several areas. "Good for the inside and the out," she'd said as she held the mug under her chin as if receiving a facial.

"I added a bunch of sugar. Figured since you drank that stuff"—she pointed to the soda—"you'd want it that way."

Gabe took a sip. "Like hot sweet tea." He smiled. "I like it."

Hattie nodded before sinking once more into the couch. "So what's next? You headed back to the hospital? You haven't told me about Bill yet."

"Oh, sorry. He was having some additional tests today for his heart. It was pretty bad, I guess. I didn't get the impression they were too worried, though. I told Gladys to call me if anything happened, but I'm headed back out there next."

They remained silent for a bit as Gabe sipped his tea. Sassy came back over and jumped into Hattie's lap where she nestled down and soon fell asleep. Maybe Gabe would visit the shelter soon. Daisy could use a friend as much as he could.

## Chapter Twenty-Three

Gabe's phone rang as he was leaving the town of Waves on his way back to the Outer Banks Hospital. Bill's number again. He clicked the button on his steering wheel to answer.

"Hello."

"Gabe? This is Pastor Tim from Cape Hatteras Baptist Church. Gladys asked me to call."

Nausea rolled through Gabe's gut. Had something gone wrong? He didn't want to think the worst, but—

"Hold on." There was a pause on the other end and then, "Here's Gladys."

"Gabe?"

"Yes, I'm here. Is Bill okay? Wait, before you say, I'm driving, and I think I should pull over." Gabe guided his truck off the road and onto the sandy beach shoulder, being careful not to go too far lest his truck get stuck. He put the truck into park and said, "Okay. Go ahead."

"The hospital decided Bill needs open heart surgery, but they can't do it here or today." Gabe could hear the weariness and stress in her voice. "They'll be transferring Bill to Sentara Heart Hospital in Norfolk in the next few minutes. I wanted to call and let you know. The surgery will wait until Monday, provided Bill is stable enough to do so. Pastor Tim is going to drive me there so I can stay with Bill."

Gabe noticed the way she gave just the basic facts. He'd been the same when telling his family about Ellie. "I'm glad Pastor Tim is with you. I'm sorry I had to leave. Daisy needed me. Plus, my sister is here now. But I'm on my way back."

"I need you to stay, actually. I need someone to run the shop and go to our house and take care of the cats."

*Run the shop? Why was Gladys worried about the shop now? Surely that should be the last thing on her mind.*

Gabe pushed down a swell of panic. "I didn't even open it today. I'm sorry." Gabe thought about the potential sales loss and felt bad for a moment. But things happen, and he'd never run the shop without Bill. "I've never run it alone, Gladys."

"I know, dear, but Bill trusts you, and he told me he's been prepping you to take over. It's okay if you just keep it closed today but try to open tomorrow because a lot of people will be heading out and need their coffee." She chuckled or sniffled. Gabe was unsure. "I know you'll do a great job. We just need it to be open. We …" She hesitated and then said, "We want to keep it open for the tourists. We already missed Friday, and Saturday is usually a good sales day. You know how those tourists get without their coffee. I need someone I can trust with the shop in case anything like this happens again," she said.

"I hope nothing like this ever happens again," Gabe countered.

She chuckled but Gabe could hear no joy in it, and this time, he definitely heard a sniffle. "And our cats will be no problem. You don't even need to go every day. Just be sure

*Changing Tides*

their litterbox is clean and check their food level. Ren is the gray one and Stimpy is the calico." Gabe smiled at the names as she proceeded to tell him where stuff was at the house, including where the secret key was kept to get inside.

"Of course. I'll get the shop open tomorrow, and I'll head over to your house right now. You don't worry about a thing. We'll get through this. You just worry about Bill and get him healthy."

"Thank you, dear. I'm going to give you back to Pastor Tim now. God bless you, Gabe."

Gabe didn't feel very blessed but accepted the offer just the same. When Pastor Tim came back on the line, Gabe said, "How is she really doing?"

"She's a strong woman. And we have a bunch of the church folks here praying. God knew she needed someone to be here and there." He laughed.

Gabe felt the need to explain. "I had to get back for my dog otherwise I wouldn't have left her."

"Oh, I know. No worries, Gabe. Gladys understands. She needs you more there—at the shop."

"I'll do whatever she needs. But I don't see why the shop can't stay closed a day or two."

"Gabe, maybe you don't know ..." The pastor hesitated for a moment, and Gabe could hear him talking in muffled tones to Gladys. "I've sent Gladys to one of the other church members to pray. You need to know something. Normally, I couldn't divulge this kind of private issue, but Gladys has called you their son, so I think she wants to tell you, but isn't sure how."

Gabe felt his stomach sink again. Perhaps Bill was dying, and they had known all along. What would he do if Bill died? He'd truly be alone again and in a new environment. He wasn't sure he could start over again.

"Bill and Gladys are barely keeping the coffee shop afloat. When you came along to rent out the apartment, they were able to pay some bills, but it's still not good. If they must close for any length of time—like for Bill's surgery and recovery which will take months—they'll lose the business. And possibly their home which they've put up as collateral."

The news punched Gabe in the gut. He'd been worried about his own life, and they were about to lose theirs. And here he'd been trying to get a discount on the rent by helping out in the shop. He felt like such a heel.

"I had no idea. Of course I'll keep it going. For as long as they need. Please be sure to tell Gladys I have it all under control."

Although he was not sure he did, Gabe intended to do his very best. It was the least he could do for these people who had offered so much. Maybe this was what God had been trying to tell him—to focus more on others instead of himself. Maybe doing so would help with his own grief.

"Great. You can call me for updates anytime. I'll text you so you have my number, and I'll try to keep you posted too."

"What about church services? Aren't you needed there?" Gabe asked partly from curiosity and partly because he'd already thought about attending services this week.

"We've another pastor who's going to fill in at least for this week, and then we'll see what happens next. Bill will probably need at least a double bypass, possibly more. They're not sure until they get in. And the recovery can be very long."

Gabe knew. His father-in-law had a double bypass years ago. Ellie had waited on him daily and pulled him through a deep depression at the time. The recovery process had taken three months just for him to get out of bed.

## Changing Tides

"Listen, Gabe, I have to get back. They're getting ready to transport Bill, and I want to pray with Bill and the crew before they go."

"Of course," said Gabe. "Please give my love to Gladys and reassure her I'll take care of everything here."

"Will do." With that, the pastor ended the call.

Gabe sat in his truck for another moment, thinking about the tasks ahead. He'd need to open the shop, but also maintain inventory and see about the money situation. Thankfully, Bill had showed him the safe combination a few weeks ago and how to make deposits at the bank. He thought about Gladys's comment that Bill had been prepping him. Had he? Gabe had thought the information was just that—information. He never considered Bill might be training him to take over.

Then he thought about the financial stress his friends were in and wondered if he could somehow help. He'd been a finance guy before he'd moved to the beach. At his last job, he'd balanced a three-million-dollar budget.

But he'd never run his own business. Although, he'd helped Ellie run hers—the numbers part anyway.

"Okay, God. Looks like you have something new in store for me. If you're standing with me, I know I can help. Give me your guidance, wisdom, and strength to do the best job I can for my friends. Let's do this."

Feeling determined, Gabe checked his rearview mirror then swung his truck back around. He'd a lot to do tonight before he could open the shop in the morning, but first he had some cats to attend to.

## Chapter Twenty-Four

After quickly dealing with Gladys and Bill's cats—he had just dumped some food and water into their bowls—he'd checked in with his sister. Cameron could work remotely and was doing so while fawning over Daisy, which suited his pup just fine.

"You'll spoil her," he'd told Cameron when she let Daisy spread out across her lap with her laptop on a table off to the side.

"Don't care. You have to deal with it when I leave, so meh." Cameron had given him a smirk then turned back to her computer.

"I'll be back up before dinner, and we can go out."

Cameron waved her hand without looking up, and Gabe went downstairs to the coffee shop. He wanted to spend a good part of his afternoon familiarizing himself with Bill's office while they were closed. That way he wouldn't have customers bothering him.

First, he checked the contents of the safe and poured over some of the finances. Pastor Tim had been right—Bill and Gladys had mortgaged their house. And they were behind in their payments to ... well, just about everyone. But Gabe had also noticed some discrepancies in the books—

miscalculations mostly—and some duplicate services Bill had been paying for and probably didn't need. Gabe set up a spreadsheet on the computer to calculate the expenses and try to determine what could be cut. By the time Bill returned, he'd have this place running in the black.

The next morning, Gabe turned the coffee shop's sign to open and turned to his sister.

"Thanks for helping. I'm not sure I could do this alone."

Cameron smiled while putting on one of the aprons. "I think I can make coffee. Probably better than you, since you don't even drink the stuff."

She turned to the coffee pots and started shoveling grounds into coffee filters like she'd been a barista her whole life. He knew the customers would appreciate her brews more than his, because his sister was a consummate coffee drinker. He would have to have her give him a tutorial before she left later that day.

"Are you sure you can't stay longer, Sis? I'm sorry we haven't had much time together."

"I really can't. I need to get back to work on Monday." She looked up and pointed a finger in his direction. "But we need to still talk about you moving back."

"I can't even consider that right now, Cam. Bill and Gladys need me to help run the shop for the foreseeable future."

She sighed, then nodded. "You were always a very loyal friend. But I want you to really think about it once things calm down. And remember, you promised to come visit for the holidays."

"I did." He ran a hand over the hair his sister had cut for him last night after a decent meal out. She'd had a few glasses of wine but seemed to have done a fine job on the cut. "But I need to help out Bill and Gladys, and I'm not sure how long that might be. So, I really can't promise to come for long." At his sister's scowl, he added, "But I promise to stay for Christmas and New Year's."

"And you will answer your texts and calls more often."

He nodded.

"And even some video chats?"

He nodded again. She drove a hard bargain, but it felt good to have her care so much. He determined to keep the bond strong with good communication with her and his parents moving forward. Their parents were aging too, and who knew how long they'd be around.

Satisfied, she turned back to her task as the door chime dinged.

Hattie shuffled into the shop, pink cane tapping. "William! It's about time you got your sorry a—" She stopped as she noticed Gabe and Cameron. "Where's Bill?"

"Have a seat, Hattie. What can I get you?" Gabe said.

"Nothing." She frowned but sat as instructed. "Now out with it."

Gabe pulled a chair over to her padded one and said, "You've met my sister, Cameron." His sister looked and smiled, then turned back to wipe the counter. Gabe turned back to Hattie. "Bill is probably going for open heart surgery on Monday at Sentara Heart Hospital in Norfolk. Pastor Tim is taking Gladys there and staying with her until after. It'll probably be, at least, a week before Bill gets released. I assume Gladys intends to stay for that time."

Hattie shook her head. "That poor thing. I hope she's holding up."

"I think her church family is taking good care of her. But she asked me to keep this place going. So here I am." Gabe spread out his hands and shrugged.

"You're a good boy." She patted his cheek. "How about some tea and a muffin?"

*Muffins. He had some leftover from Gladys's last batch but what would he do when they ran out?*

He rose to fill her order, but Hattie put a hand on his arm. "Wait ... do you have muffins? What are you feedin' folks?"

Gabe sat back down. "We have a few muffins ... I think. Although, I'm not much of a cook or baker, I'll need to figure something out. Thankfully, most people go for the pastries and not the more complicated stuff Bill likes to make. I've told him he should give that up, but he insists people need a solid breakfast."

"Like those double decker bacon sandwiches I saw you eating the other day are healthy." Hattie's sarcasm came as quickly as her frown.

"I can bake some items before I leave," said his sister. "I think I saw some recipes around here somewhere, or I can look a few up on the internet."

Hattie nodded then tapped her cane as she then leaned forward to stand. Gabe took hold of her elbow and helped.

"I'll be off to the store then to get supplies. You got an oven back there, right?" Gabe nodded, and she turned for the door. "We'll get this place in tiptop shape in no time. Thank goodness today's Saturday. The tourists are mostly leaving right now so we've time to get some stuff baked before the new crop arrives. I'm off like a herd of turtles!"

Later that day, Cameron and Hattie had baked several batches of banana and chocolate chip muffins. Hattie hadn't been able to find any blueberries at the store. After they had stored some of the baked goods in the fridge, Cameron cleaned up the kitchen area while Gabe took stock of the other inventory. He'd be well suited for Monday when the bulk of tourists came in to start their week. What he'd do after that, he was unsure. But his sister had printed out some recipes and found a few of Gladys's so he'd work from those. Hattie had agreed to help as much as she could.

When there was no more to do for this day, Cameron wiped her hands on her apron and then, after untying it, handed it to Gabe. "I need to get going."

Daisy jumped up from her blankets and came to Cameron's side.

"I thought you were going to wait until tomorrow. You've only been here one day."

"You don't answer calls or texts for weeks, but now, you want me to stay?" She offered him a scowl while petting Daisy's head. "I've had so much coffee, I think I wouldn't be able to sleep tonight anyway. Plus, this way I can wake up and be fresh for tomorrow. Paul texted to remind me we have a birthday party to go to."

Gabe threw the apron into the pile of laundry to be cleaned. "I understand. I'm so glad you came. I don't know what I would have done without you. I'm still not sure. I really hope Bill comes home soon."

"Well, you're going to have to lean on me now," chimed in Hattie from her spot by the counter as she waited on the last customer of the day. "I'm not as good of a baker as Gladys or this young thing, but I got a few tricks up my sleeve." She winked at a little boy and his father who had come in a few minutes prior as she handed them chocolate chip muffins in a bag. They waved and turned to the door. Gabe followed behind and turned the sign to closed.

His sister pulled Gabe into a hug. "I'll go get my things and then be off." She pulled back and pointed a finger at his face. "Keep in touch better, or I'll be making more surprise visits. Or dragging you home."

Gabe put his hands up in surrender. "Yes, ma'am."

"And get those boxes unpacked if you're staying. It looks like a frat house up there."

Gabe agreed again.

A few minutes later, he watched Cameron walk to her car while Daisy stood at the door and whined. Gabe immediately felt a sense of loss at her going too. He'd not realized how much he'd missed her.

"She's a good egg," said Hattie as she wiped off the counter, then walked to the sink. "I'll clean up these dishes then be out of your hair."

"Oh no, you don't." Gabe pulled the rag from her hand and turned to shuffle her to the door, Daisy hot on their heels. "You've been on your feet all day, and I know that's probably bothering you. I'll clean up here, and you get home and rest."

"Well, I never—" But Hattie smiled as she grabbed her cane and let him lead her to the door. "I'll be back bright and early on Monday to help."

"Get here when you can, I appreciate it."

Before he could shut the door, Hattie turned back and said, "Gabriel, mind if we give the Lord some thanks before I skedaddle?"

"Of course not." Why hadn't he thought of that sooner? He was so out of the habit, he'd need to cultivate it again.

Hattie stepped back inside and grabbed his hands. As she began to give praise to God for the good things of the day, Gabe's chest warmed. It felt good to pray again, to seek God in all things, and to praise him, even in the midst of the hard things. He hadn't even known she was a God-fearing woman.

*Changing Tides*

"And thank you, Lord Jesus, for this young man who came to help Bill and Gladys. You knew what they needed and have set your plan in motion. We can rest easy knowing you have this whole mess in hand, Lord. You're the great rock and the master of our lives, and we're so mighty thankful. Amen."

When she let go of his hands, Hattie looked up into his eyes and smiled. He smiled back, awed at her words. He'd only come here to escape his grief. Had God known all along he'd help these folks or had he simply used Gabe's disobedience and turned it for his good? He'd probably never know. But he felt God moving in some way here, making good come even from a bad situation—Bill's heart attack.

Hattie patted his hand then turned again. "Whew! Hotter than blue blazes out here."

Gabe smiled, then locked the door behind her and watched until she'd gotten into her car and eased the gigantic beast across the street.

Turning back to the shop, he found he felt tired but also invigorated. Before tackling the dishes, he sat down in the plush chair. Daisy jumped into his lap and began smothering him with kisses. Today had been a good day. He hoped it had been for Bill and Gladys too.

## Chapter Twenty-Five

After both ladies left, Gabe cleaned up the shop with Daisy's help—he the dishes and she the floor with her ever-searching snout. When everything was clean and ready for Monday, he turned to Daisy and said, "Let's go eat, girl. I'm starving."

Upstairs, Gabe fed Daisy the standard kibble and added a bit of shredded cheese from the burrito he made for himself. Tomorrow, he would have to touch base again with Brent and ask for an extended bit of time off from the grocery store. Although the coffee shop was only open until three o'clock each day, by the time he cleaned up and did the financial stuff, he didn't have much time for another job. At least until Bill was back on his feet.

Gabe took his burrito and sat down at the small kitchen table to eat. Daisy looked up from her bowl, and he smiled. "Yeah, I know. Looks weird, doesn't it. But I think it's time I put this table to some use."

Gabe tucked into his burrito but soon stopped with a fork halfway to his mouth as a thought became clear in his mind. He would quit the grocery job. He really didn't need it. If Bill had intended for him to take over, he'd need all his time in the coffee shop anyway.

## Sue A. Fairchild

With that settled in his mind, he finished his burrito and put the dirty plate into the sink for washing later.

Gabe peered into his fridge and realized he'd need more groceries soon too. Grabbing a pen and ripping the corner from a discarded envelope, he began a list of food items. Bill was right, he needed to take better care of himself. He'd be a role model for his friend, and together, they'd begin a new phase of their lives.

He thought about the Bible story Bill had told him about Moses. He was holding up his friends' arms now for this battle ... why hadn't he ever let them do the same to help him?

He'd not heard from Gladys or Pastor Tim today but knew it had probably been a long day. He'd touch base with Tim tomorrow—maybe he'd even go to church.

As he moved into the living room, he considered if he wanted to dig more into the books from the shop or take a little time to chill. He thought then of his sister nagging him about the boxes. He could start unpacking those. He walked out of the kitchen and into the living room and saw a little envelope sitting on the coffee table. He moved to it and saw his sister's handwriting.

> I'm sorry I couldn't give this to you in person, but I wasn't sure you'd want Hattie to see and there was never a good time. I should have given this to you earlier, but ... it just didn't happen. If you read it and need me, I'm only a phone call away.

He tore open the envelope to see what she might have left behind. Surely she hadn't left him money for her stay? But when he saw the different handwriting inside, Gabe's heart nearly stopped.

Ellie's looping script nearly burst off the page. He'd not seen her handwriting in more than a year. Who wrote letters these days? The note on lined paper was dated more than a year ago ... before her death. He hesitated a moment, wondering if this would send him down another spiral. He'd done well recently and had barely thought of Ellie yesterday or today while busy with Bill, Gladys, and the shop. In fact, he'd barely grieved yesterday—the anniversary of her death—because of the current situations going on in his life. For a moment, he felt bad, as if he'd forgotten her. But he knew that was not true. He'd simply been going on with life. Ellie would have wanted that, wouldn't she?

He took a deep breath and began to read.

> My love,
> I know this note probably comes as a shock to you because if you're reading it, it means I've left you for the next world. Weird to hear from a dead person, isn't it? I know I said I would come back to haunt you so you wouldn't be lonely, but I couldn't be sure God would allow that, so I did this instead. Cameron agreed to give this to you only if you were not coping well after my death. She might have shared it no matter what ... she always does what she wants, so I'm not sure. But if she did wait ... thank her for me.
> While I'm writing this, I'm very sick and feel like the end is near.

Gabe stopped reading for a moment and choked back a sob. Ellie had always had a penchant for writing. Seeing her words now made him realize how much he truly missed her voice.

After pulling the tissue box closer, he focused once more on this unusual letter.

> You have been such a great husband, and I need you to know it. I'm not sure I ever told you enough. You have done so much for me in this hard time—through every hard time we ever had. You've been my Aaron and Hur.

Gabe stopped reading again. Was this a coincidence that Ellie referenced the same Bible story he'd been thinking about and Bill had reminded him of just the other day? "No such thing as coincidence," he and Ellie had always said. He shook his head and turned back to the email.

> But I know you don't think you've done enough. And I know you're going to beat yourself up after my death, wondering if you did enough or if there was anything you should have done to make me happier. But know this—I was immensely happy with you. IMMENSELY. When God gave me you, I felt like I had won the lottery. I praised him for you every day. And even though I'm gone sooner than we expected, I don't want you to blame God.

She knew him so well. He couldn't believe what he was reading. It was as if she'd looked right into his soul from heaven and written this letter. But she'd written it *before* her death. He shook his head, not believing how she could have thought this far ahead while enduring the pain she was in at the end.

> I know what you'll do. Revert back to your bachelor ways. Let me guess ... cold elbow noodles in the fridge with spaghetti sauce that you put on top, like a sad version of spaghetti. No wait! Salsa. You put that stuff on everything.

She really *did* know him. He laughed but then sobered. He'd forgotten how much he missed her. Her voice came through so much in this letter—she'd always been a good writer.

> I know you probably reverted and are probably beating yourself up. I can see you living that hermit life you always said you would if I died first. But I want to ask you to NOT do that. By now, it has probably been about a year since my death. You have grieved enough. Time to pull up those big boy

*pants and move on. Or, at least, take a step outside. Invite in a friend. Call your sister. Take a trip. Get back to church. But don't wallow in your grief.*
*Remember when I would get down on myself and you would say, "How long are you going to wallow?"*
*Well? How long, Gabe?*
*Now, I could be completely wrong. Maybe my death has released you from some kind of prison, and you have been living the carefree life. If so, I'll be rejoicing in heaven to see it. (Yes, I know that's not true. I'll be with God, so I'll not care about you or your life anymore. Sorry. It's the truth. I still love you, but the streets up there are made with GOLD. I mean ...)*

He laughed again. Only Ellie would point out this fact. They had both cringed when people said their loved ones were looking down on them from heaven. Although a comforting notion ... not biblical or rational.

"I hope my mom isn't looking down on me," Ellie had said when her mom died. "She spent too many years worrying about me here on earth. And now she has a whole new, healthy body. I hope she's enjoying it!"

Gabe realized that Ellie had gained the same thing—a new, healthy body. She was healed in heaven and could probably go to the beach every day if she wanted. Maybe she lived on a beach there. Or maybe heaven was so warm and lovely all over that she didn't need to.

He longed to be with her there but knew God still had plans for him here. Plans to help Bill and Gladys especially.

He turned back to the letter.

*Anyway ... don't wallow. Yes, this isn't how we wanted life to be, but it's this way, and you must cope. I pray you will find friends or loved ones who will help you. I pray you won't sequester yourself away from people or do something dumb in your grief. (I better not see you in heaven for a really long time, mister.) Because whether you believe it or not, we need people.*

"I need you, Ellie. I only ever needed you."

*Every human longs for connection. You can't live a good life without it. Now you can certainly be introverted when you need to be but don't shut everyone out. Let someone in. Please. Okay. Enough of my nagging. I bet you missed this. Not. But I love you so much, and I only want the best things for you. I can't be there to give them to you, but I know you will find a way to go on. And if you have not yet, I hope this letter encourages you do to so.*
*I love you now and forever,*
*Ellie*

    Gabe read the letter once more as he continuously wiped tears from his eyes. Daisy had come to lie beside him on the floor and kept looking up at him with her saddest look. Oh, how he loved Ellie. How special she'd been to think of him in her last moments. How wonderful their love and marriage had been. He'd thought for the last year that it was impossible to go on without her, and yet, he had.

    And now he had friends who had come into his life despite his grumpy attitude and penchant for shutting people out. Despite wanting to live closed off from the world and focus on his grief, God had brought people into his life that he knew Gabe would begin to care about. And he had. He cared about Bill, Gladys, and even Hattie. These folks were his family now. And in order to help them, he needed to stop being so selfish.

    Refolding the letter, he decided to call Pastor Tim for an update.

    "I'm not going to wallow any longer, Ellie. You're right. It's time to start living life again."

## Chapter Twenty-six

Gabe woke the next morning with Pastor Tim's good news at the forefront of his mind. Bill had weathered the trip to Sentara Heart Hospital in Norfolk well and would have his surgery tomorrow morning. Recovery would be difficult as with any open-heart surgery, but he'd probably be home within the week.

Gabe knew he had God to thank. He thought of the many folks praying for Bill and Gladys and how Hattie had prayed last night.

He needed to get back to church. When he'd inquired of Pastor Tim last night about services, he'd told Gabe the morning service started at eleven. It was now only six. Gabe quickly made his decision and leapt from the bed. After taking Daisy for a quick walk to do her business, he rummaged through an unopened box of clothes and found his one pair of flipflops and swim trunks. If he hurried, he could beat the newly arrived tourists and enjoy the sunrise.

At the door, he said, "Not this time, Daisy, but I promise we'll go more often." She whined but stayed put.

He found the easier route to the beach that he and Daisy had found a few days ago. When he crested the small dune, the beach spread out before him without a single soul touching its shores. The sun had begun its ascent and washed the sand with reds and oranges as Gabe strode to the surf's edge.

Shucking his flip-flops, he ventured into the waves, biting back a sharp inhale at the cool morning water. He moved slowly as his body adjusted to the temperature. He'd hoped it would still be warm, but this early in the morning he couldn't expect bath water temps.

When the water reached his thighs, he dove into the surf. The water sluicing over him reminded Gabe how much he loved playing in the ocean. Why hadn't he done so since coming to live here? He broke the surface and was able to stand once more and let his body relax into the next wave.

"Go with the flow," Nora had said.

*Yes. That's what I need to do. I want to be free again.*

He'd once told Ellie this was his happy place—in the water, letting it wash over and move him without effort. *I like it because I'm free. I don't have to think about much, the water does the work. The buoyancy of the waves gives me a light feeling.*

He'd not felt light since Ellie's death. For a moment, guilt rose in him, but then it washed away as he dove again into the surf.

When he took in his next bit of fresh, salty air, he thought of how the beach had been Ellie's favorite place because of the sun and the warmth. But it was also his favorite place because of the water and this feeling of buoyancy. Daily, he'd tried so hard to be connected to the earth, grounded, solid, serious ... but true happiness came from letting go and just floating along with the tide.

It felt like a metaphor for a relationship with God. In the ocean, you could still be connected to the earth—the water surrounding you in its protective embrace, the waves moving you around without much effort. When you gave in to the motion, you could feel peace and still also feel secure.

That was how he needed to be with God. To allow the Lord to direct his life didn't mean to be led about like a puppet but to be wrapped in his ever-loving embrace. God was secure. He worked all things out for our good. He was always with us. He'd never leave us. Even now Gabe felt how he'd directed this move—despite Gabe thinking it had been all his doing.

Gabe smiled as he made his way back to the shore. He could never forget Ellie and didn't want to, but what he needed to do was let the grief go. Maybe it would take more time, but he could start today by choosing to make new choices.

Shivering now and wishing he'd brought a towel, he grabbed up his flip-flops and made for home. His first step into reclaiming his relationship with God would be getting back to church and getting into God's Word.

Daisy had not been happy he was going again so soon after leaving her for the beach. She'd become used to Gabe being away all day—not coming and going. He wondered again about finding a companion for her. He'd have to check out the rescue center as soon as he had time. And he'd start taking Daisy on longer walks in the evening too.

Which meant quitting his job at the grocery store. He'd try to talk to Brent today.

He pulled down on the neck of his shirt as he slowed behind a few cars turning into Connor's Supermarket. He'd had to rummage through some boxes of clothes before finding his button-down shirts and dress slacks—items he'd not needed since moving to the beach. Living at the beach did have one advantage ... he rarely needed to dress up. After fifteen long years in the corporate world, he'd grown weary of restricting necklines and ties. But he'd donned both this morning for his return to church. He hoped he wasn't overdressed, though.

He thought how proud his sister would be when he texted her later to tell her he'd cleared out one box. Most of it had been the clothes he rarely wore—dress and beach clothes. He'd put some into drawers or hung in the closet, and the rest he'd put back into the box to donate.

He slowed again when the church sign came into view, then pulled into the paved driveway and parking lot. He'd come early but cars already filled most of the spaces. He opted for a space in the back of the church where there was more room for his big truck.

Wiping his hands over his pants, he stared through the windshield at the other parishioners entering the building. Some wore dress clothes, but far more sported standard beach attire—khaki shorts and colorful, button-down shirts. He'd be out of place. Before he could talk himself out of attending, he pushed himself from the truck and approached the front door.

An older woman with gray hair greeted him as she stuck out a bulletin. "Good morning! Welcome. Have you been here before?" He shook his head and she continued, "If you would please sign our visitor's register, we'd appreciate it. How did you hear about our church?"

"I know Bill and Gladys Brower."

The woman's face lit up. "Oh! You must be Gabe! Pastor Tim mentioned you might stop in today." She ushered him forward. "I'm thankful you're here, Gabe."

*Changing Tides*

He wondered how Tim might have assumed he'd come today, but then remembered he'd asked the pastor about service times. Still, it felt odd to be recognized when he preferred to blend into the crowd. Maybe coming to Bill's church wasn't such a great idea after all.

As he was considering seat choices—next to a family of four or between two older couples—he felt a slap on his back.

"Gabe! Glad to see you."

He turned to see Brent, his boss from the store.

He cringed. This guy was a Christian? "I didn't know you came ... that you went to church."

Brent nodded. "Not too many Baptist churches on the island, and this one is the closest to Avon. Here"—he pointed toward a pew—"come sit with me."

Gabe felt again like the proverbial heel at not knowing his boss better. Maybe there was a reason he acted so ... ridiculous around women. Maybe he hadn't had friends to show him proper etiquette.

"I like this church," Brent said, then leaned in to whisper. "There are a lot of young single women. And they have a singles group on Thursdays." He sat back and winked.

*Okay. Maybe he was just an idiot.*

"Brent, who's this?"

Gabe looked up at a middle-aged woman glaring down at him.

"This is Gabe, Mom. This is his first time here." Brent grabbed Gabe's elbow, making him rise to let the woman into the pew.

"Good to meet you, Gabe." She squinted at him as she passed. "Are you one of Brent's *friends* from the bar?"

"No, Mom. Gabe works at the store." Brent sat back down and rolled his eyes at Gabe. "He's a widower who just moved here a couple of months ago."

Gabe opened his mouth to speak, but Brent's mother interrupted.

"Brent had a girl once." She smoothed out her skirt as she looked past her son to Gabe. "Was engaged. But she took off with a surfboarder."

He rolled his eyes. "Cliché, right? But I'm better off." Brent puffed up his chest, but his mother pushed him back so she could talk to Gabe again.

"That hussy hurt my baby bad." She looked at Brent and scowled. "Started hanging around bars and loose women since then."

"Mom!" Brent glanced around the sanctuary. "Can you keep it down?"

His mother smoothed her hair this time, and said, "It's a defense mechanism if you ask me." She looked Gabe up and down then. "Maybe you're a nice boy who could straighten him out."

"Maybe we could get a beer sometime and talk about it," Gabe said to Brent.

His mother scowled again, but Brent turned to him with wide eyes and a slack jaw. He looked down at his hands and said, "Yeah. I'd like that. I don't have too many friends."

Gabe patted his shoulder as the piano player sat down to play the prelude. "The least I can do for making me feel welcome, brother."

Gabe turned his attention to the bulletin until the worship leader stood up with a guitar and invited them to sing along. The church was small like his last church but looked like it'd been recently painted. The piano gleamed at the front of the sanctuary and a television was mounted beyond the pulpit. Gabe smoothed a hand over his Bible and pushed back a surge of nervousness.

The songs were a mix of old and new, some Gabe knew, and some he didn't. For the next hour, he relaxed into the familiar rhythm of the church service. He'd missed being part of a family of believers and couldn't wait until he could share this time with Bill and Gladys every Sunday.

## Chapter Twenty-Seven

Gabe had declined lunch with Brent and his mother, telling them he needed to get back to the shop to do some more work before tomorrow. He felt bad but told Brent they would get together soon. He also told Brent he quit, which upset his boss, but then he said he understood. As Gabe made his way to the Brower's house to check on Ren and Stimpy, he felt hunger pangs. He was surprised his appetite had seemed to come back overnight. After grabbing a quick bite to eat at a little food shack, he continued to their home.

The house was a simple ranch home with white siding and set up on stilts like most of the other homes on the island. Facing the street was a wooden deck with a wooden glider. Gabe envisioned Bill and Gladys sitting out here every night and watching the neighborhood. The house was quiet as he let himself in.

From the front door, Gabe could see through to the living room and to large sliding glass doors. He'd not noticed much the last time he'd been here, in a hurry to get in and out. The kitchen, where the cats' food bowls sat, was to the right. But before tending to the cats right away, Gabe felt something telling him to look around. He didn't want to snoop, but he moved to the glass doors and peered out into the bay.

The view was spectacular and seemed to stretch on, almost as far as the ocean. Choppy waves crested across its surface.

He pulled open the door and breathed in the fresh air. Different on this side of the island and not as salty, but still fresh and crisp. A small deck hugged the back of the house with two Adirondack chairs on either side of the door. Why had he never come to visit Bill here? If he'd known about this peaceful spot, he might have come sooner.

Once again, Gabe thought about how he wanted to do things differently.

He noticed a bit of the railing had come loose, and the steps leading down to the bay were blocked off due to a few missing steps. He pushed at the railing and realized too late how wobbly it was. Gabe found himself lying on the sand, inches from a very prickly looking bush. He stood and brushed himself off as he looked back up at the railing. Sure enough, it had broken free just where he'd stood. He'd bring out some tools later today and fix it. He climbed back up the steps to the deck, being careful not to put too much weight on any and, stepping over the broken ones, went back inside.

As he looked around the house some more, he saw more things that needed repair. An overhead light whose cover was broken, a few tiles in the bathroom that had cracked or were missing altogether, and a chair with a broken arm in the living room. Yet the place looked and smelled fresh and clean. Gladys had done her best, he could tell, but the strain on their finances had kept them from repairing even the simplest items. He vowed to dig out his tools and get to work on everything that needed to be done as soon as Bill was settled.

He moved back into the bathroom and checked the litterboxes. As he cleaned, Stimpy ventured out from under the bed to smell his hand.

"Hey, little guy. Where's your friend?" He stroked the cat's head, and he purred. "I got to get this place fixed up for you guys and your parents."

He stood and caught a quick flash of gray out of the corner of his eye. The mass had fled into the closet. He stepped closer and gently pushed open the door. There backed up against a pile of clothes was Ren. The gray cat hissed and snarled, and Gabe held up his hands.

"Okay, little guy. Don't mean any harm. Just wanted to be sure you were okay."

Gabe backed away slowly and finished the task with the litterbox.

Next, he moved to the kitchen and washed his hands. He pulled down the kibble from above the fridge and refilled the cat's bowls. They had not eaten much, and Gabe wondered how they would fare if Gladys and Bill were gone much longer. Maybe he should move them to his house for the time being.

But no, that would be too much of a disruption. Especially for Ren, it seemed. Better to leave them be.

Gabe took a quick look in the fridge and made a mental note to talk to Pastor Tim later today about having some food brought in by church members for when Bill returned. Maybe Hattie would even make some things. She seemed to be willing and ready to help.

Having done his duty for the day, Gabe checked around to be sure he'd not forgotten anything and ventured back out to his truck. He'd grab some tools at home and come back later to fix that railing and start making a list of other items he could tackle until Bill came home.

## Chapter Twenty-Eight

When Gabe returned home about an hour later, Daisy gave him a sniffing inspection.

"Yes, girl, I'll introduce you to Ren and Stimpy soon."

Gabe moved to the bedroom where he kept the unpacked boxes, hoping he could find some of his tools and head back to Gladys's and Bill's. Daisy followed with her purple rhino in her mouth and lay down next to the boxes as if to say, "Let's do this."

He opened the first box, but it was mostly filled with books. He took a few out he wanted to read and placed them on his nightstand. The remainder he pulled out and stacked on a pile next to the bed. *Note to self: buy bookshelf.*

In the next box, he found some fancy kitchenware—their wedding champagne glasses and a few crystal items they'd received for wedding gifts. Gabe studied the etching on the glasses for a moment before carefully rolling them back into the tissue and repacking them. He'd need to think about what to do with them later. In the next box were the tools he had wanted to find. He knew some of his larger ones were still in the truck. He picked up the box and moved it out to the living room by the front door where he could grab it easily tomorrow.

Moving back into the bedroom and to the next box, he flipped open the lid and inhaled a sharp breath. Their wedding album, Ellie's preserved bouquet, and some framed photos of the two of them together. Gabe pulled out a framed photo first—one of them laughing while dancing with each other. *My uncle and aunt's wedding anniversary party.* It had been one of the first family functions he'd taken Ellie to, and she'd fit right in. He looked so happy in the photo, and she was laughing with her head against his shoulder.

Gabe choked back a sob and sat down hard on the floor. Daisy immediately came to him and nuzzled his arm. He pushed her aside, and she whined but lay back down on the carpet.

He pulled out another framed photo, one of them with Daisy on a back country road. Ellie had convinced him to have professional photos taken and to include the rambunctious dog. He laughed as he remembered how hard it had been to get Daisy to cooperate. But you'd never know it from this photo. They looked like the perfect little happy family walking down the country lane. In the next framed photo, he and Ellie stood against a tree in their wedding outfits. Ellie had looked so lovely that day. To him, she looked beautiful every day, but that day she'd outdone herself. He traced a finger over her face in the photo. She'd not overdone her makeup or gone for some crazy hairstyle that wasn't her but had just enhanced her normal beauty.

*I miss you so much.*

Gabe let the tears fall as he pulled out the album and the other items. He'd find a special place for them all. Then, at the bottom, he found a small box full of papers. At first, he thought they were just random cards, but then, he realized they were every card he'd ever given Ellie. As he pulled out each one, he realized she'd dated them and even added some notes to a few. Then he found a few notes friends had written to them on their wedding day.

*We all know this is right,* wrote one friend.

*You met because of me,* wrote another.

*May you have many, many blessed years together,* wrote another.

Gabe fell back against the bed and let the tears come in earnest now. They hadn't had many years together, but the ones they'd had were beyond special. Ellie had been more than just a wife—she'd been his helpmeet, his confidante, his friend.

After a few minutes of letting himself cry, he replaced the items in the box and moved on to the last one. Inside, he found a jewelry box with some of his favorite pieces of Ellie's inside and a stack of notebooks. Her notebooks. Her words written in her hand. He opened one and read the first page. She'd written about her own self-doubts, fears of losing Gabe, and trying to figure out who God wanted her to be.

> *How can I be a good wife to Gabe if I have so many doubts about myself? How can I keep him from leaving me like every other person has? God, help me be a good wife. Help me resolve my own issues so I can be the best partner Gabe deserves.*

Gabe closed the notebook and brought it to his lips, kissing it lightly. Then he gathered up the journals and moved them to his nightstand, pushing some of his books aside. He'd read a little of Ellie's words every night and some of the books he loved. That way he would never forget her but would also be moving forward too.

*Life is about finding a balance after all.*

## Chapter Twenty-nine

Gabe opened the shop on Monday with Hattie by his side. As the day wore on, he noticed the pronounced hitch in her step and tried to get her to sit as much as possible. But the old woman was tenacious and seemed to have the energy of someone a quarter her age as they served a bevy of new tourists.

As predicted, most of them opted for the baked goods over any cooked items, for which Gabe was grateful. Cooking sandwiches took up time, and customers often backed up in the meantime. Plus, their supply was dwindling. He didn't intend to buy any more than he had to for stuff that wasn't selling.

By noon, the crowd had dissipated, and Hattie plopped down in her padded chair for a much-needed rest.

"Lord a mercy," she said, using a napkin to wipe her top lip. "That was land office business this morning."

"Yeah, but I'm noticing on most days, the crowd dies off before noon. Do you know if that's normally the case?"

Hattie fanned herself with her napkin. "I guess so. Since Bill doesn't really offer food other than breakfast sandwiches, the tourists go to the other restaurants."

Gabe had been thinking about how to make business more profitable for the last two days. There were many things that didn't seem to be working, but he'd have to pay more attention on a day-by-day basis. "I think we might be able to close sooner."

"But then you would miss the afternoon sales—however sparse they may be."

Hattie had a point, but did the afternoon sales justify staying open until two o'clock each day? Gabe wasn't sure. But they had to find a way to make the business more sound.

Gabe wondered how Bill's open-heart surgery was going. Pastor Tim had called last night to say Bill was mostly stable, and the surgery would take place sometime today, then texted about an hour ago to say it was go time. Since the surgery was last minute, Bill might have to wait for other surgeries to be done first. And the doctor only did so many a day as they were long and complicated procedures. Tim told him the surgery would probably be at least four hours long. There would still be a long road ahead, but hospitals and insurance dictate how long patients can stay in their care, so Gabe figured Bill would be home by the next weekend if all went well.

How he longed to hug Gladys and listen to Bill's chiding. He'd missed it these last few days. Gladys reminded him a bit of his grandmother, whom he'd not hugged since well before her death. His family didn't do hugs that much, but Ellie had, and he missed them. She'd convinced him early on that hugs meant more than kisses and even sex.

Hattie patted his arm now breaking him of his reverie. "I need to get going—these old bones are feeling the strain today. What else do you need?"

Gabe glanced at the clock. Maybe he'd close for the day.

"Head home. I think I'll close for the day. People are out on the beach anyway, and I can do a few things before heading over to Gladys and Bill's to do some work."

After Hattie left and he'd locked the door, he bounded up the stairs to his apartment. Daisy greeted him as usual, and he told her, "Want to go see some kitties?" He knew the dog couldn't understand him, yet her excitement seemed to grow. He grabbed her leash and led her downstairs and into his truck. He added a few more tools to the back and drove out to their house.

When Gabe opened the door to the Brower's house, Daisy sprinted inside, nose to the ground. He saw a flash of brown dart under the couch. Daisy must have seen it too because she bolted toward the cat and put her nose under the couch. A short yelp came next, and Daisy sat back on her haunches. She shook her head and sneezed.

"Got ya, did he? You need to play nice, Daisy. Give Stimpy some room." He tugged at her collar, and she abandoned the couch in search of other treasure. Gabe heard a growl from under the piece of furniture. "Yeah, yeah. I hear ya, Stimp. She's moved on. Relax."

Gabe moved to the bathroom and quickly cleaned out the litterboxes again, being careful not to spread too much litter on the floor. Daisy came to see what he was doing, and he shooed her away. Ren came out from under the bed and let Daisy sniff him, but then retreated just as quickly. When Daisy tried to crawl under the bed with the cat, Gabe pulled at her collar again.

"Leave it. This is a slow process, Daisy, but if we want to adopt a kitty of our own, you need to get some practice." He was not sure Daisy was on board with the whole kitten thing, but he'd thought it over and determined it was what he wanted. She'd have to deal. And he hoped being around the Brower's cats for now would ease her into the idea.

As Gabe was going for his tools to try to fix the broken light, his phone rang.

He pulled it from his pocket and saw Pastor Tim's number.

"Hey, Pastor, is Bill done already? That was a quick—"

"Gabe. Please let me speak."

Gabe shut his mouth as the happy feeling he had just a minute earlier washed away with the tide.

"I hate to make this call, Gabe, but Gladys asked me to let you know." The pastor paused and Gabe wished he'd just say it. He knew what was coming anyway. He could hear the sense of loss in Tim's tone. "Gabe, Bill is gone. He had a massive heart attack as they were getting into his chest. They weren't fast enough to save him."

Gabe sunk to the floor. *No, no, no, no—*

"Gabe, are you there?"

His stomach roiled, and he pushed his hand to his mouth. Gulping a breath, he said, "Yes. I-I'm here."

"Gladys is obviously very torn up about this. We need to make some arrangements here, but then we'll be bringing her home. Can you be sure everything is ready at the house? Maybe get her some food?"

Gabe was nodding his head, but then realized Tim couldn't see him. "Yes, yes. I'll do that. I'm actually at their house right now. Yes, I'll make sure. When will you get here?"

"I'm not sure. Probably late. Don't feel like you need to stick around. It will be a long drive back, but I think she wants to be home. I'll call you when we're on our way."

Gabe thanked the pastor and hung up. He felt numb. Daisy had come to his side and seemed to sense his distress. She whined now and put her head in his lap.

*Not again. Why when I finally begin to feel again does this happen?*

He couldn't even remember what he'd said to Bill last. Had his friend known how much he appreciated him? Gabe felt horrible for being a crappy friend in the little time he'd had with Bill. If he'd only known.

No. He had to stop this. He had said the same thing with Ellie. If he'd only known. But we *do* know. Life is but a vapor. We don't know what tomorrow will bring. God told his people we should live as if today is our last. So why did he keep thinking life would go on forever?

He pushed himself to his feet. He'd not make this mistake again. Gladys needed him now, and he'd see to it that she never wanted for anything again. And he'd get that cat. And he'd go to the beach. And he'd determine what *he* wanted ... needed.

As he made his way to the door, he collapsed again against the wall.

*Oh, Bill. My friend. I'm so sorry. I failed you like I failed Ellie, but I'll make it up to you. I'll take care of Gladys, I promise.*

Then Gabe realized who he should really be talking to. He moved back into the house and knelt in front of the sliding glass doors.

"God ... God, I don't know what to say. I want to blame you, but I know you warned us about this temporal life. And yet ... why did you have to take Bill so soon when I was just starting to befriend him? When I was just starting to let him in."

As he often did in times of the most intense pain, he heard Ellie's voice in his head. *It's not only about you.*

He nodded. "Yes, Lord. I see. There are many stories at play, not just my own. You know the greater picture, and I don't." A sob choked him, and Gabe let the tears come. He bent over and pushed his face into the carpet as the sobs racked his body.

After he'd released some of his grief, he sat upright again. "Lord, use me. Show me your way. I don't want to control my life on my own anymore. I need your guidance. And your strength. Gladys needs your strength now, Lord. Let me help her. Show me how, God. Show me."

Gabe stayed in that position until the sun set across the bay. Ellie and Bill and all the others had been right. The sunsets were beautiful here. As he watched the reds, blues, oranges, and hints of purple fade away, he knew his life would be forever different once more. But this time, he'd not wallow in his grief. He'd use what he'd learned to help Gladys and others. He'd start anew once more.

## Chapter Thirty

As the sun set, Gabe realized he'd told Tim he'd ready the house. He stood and went to the fridge. Not much lay inside and what did was nearly spoiled. He spent a few minutes combing through and discarding the unusable items and then made a quick list on his phone of some staples Gladys would need.

If she were anything like him, she'd not want to eat much during this time. He remembered those first days without Ellie—lack of sleep and nutrition. He vaguely remembered his sister being there, but not much else. While he had his phone out, he texted Cameron to give her the news and then strode to his truck with Daisy in tow.

"I'll drop you off at the house first, girl. Gladys needs some alone time right now, not some dog hounding her heels."

After he'd dropped Daisy back at his apartment, he drove to the Food Lion. Brent spotted him almost immediately.

"Gabe! Did you hear?"

Gabe nodded as he tried to push past his boss. "Yes, Tim asked me to grab some groceries. They'll be back soon, so I really need to go."

Brent backed out of the way, but then called after him, "Tell Sonja at register one that I said everything you have is on the house!"

Gabe gave a thumbs up, then yelled, "Thank you." He'd planned to pay for the items himself, of course, but whatever worked.

After filling a basket with milk, bread, some fruit, and even a Entenmann's crumb cake—not up to Gladys' standards but it would do—he went to register one. Brent must have already been here because Sonja simply bagged the items without ringing them through.

"Don't you need to ring it in for inventory?" he asked.

"You don't have much. I'll remember. Just go."

He thanked her and moved quickly back to his truck. He was beginning to see that neighbors on a small island really did look out for one another. He thought of how his neighbors had called the cops when they thought his house had been broken into and now the love and support from these folks for Gladys. Yes, this was the kind of support system he needed. The kind of community he wanted to be part of.

When he arrived back at the house, two other cars sat in the driveway, and lights lit up the interior. Anxiety pinched Gabe's gut. He could certainly get groceries and fix broken items, but being a supportive listening ear would be difficult. Could he separate his own grief from hers?

Feeling unsure, he grabbed the bag of groceries and moved to the front door. Should he knock or just walk in? As he debated, the front window curtain moved and suddenly the front door opened.

"Gabe. I wasn't sure if I should call you or wait," said Pastor Tim as he ushered him inside. "Gladys is lying down in her bedroom for a bit, but she was feeling hungry. I noticed you cleaned out some items." He grabbed the bag from Gabe and moved to the kitchen where a woman stood washing some plates. "Gabe, this is my wife, Sara."

Gabe and the woman smiled at one another as she took the bag from her husband. "Oh, bread and cold meat. Good. I can make her a sandwich."

Gabe watched as the pastor's wife moved about the kitchen with ease, and he wondered if the couple had been here before or if she was simply accustomed to working in strange kitchens.

"What can I do?" Gabe asked.

"Um … how about you boys make some lemonade?" Sara said. "I think there is some of that mix stuff in the cupboard there." She pointed, and Gabe obeyed.

Tim pulled out a pitcher and filled it as Gabe read the instructions. As the two men went about their task, Gabe's anxiety began to rise. He felt grief over Bill as well but would stuff it for Gladys. Yet could he keep his grief about Ellie at bay? Now was not the time to wallow in his grief, he needed to be strong for Gladys.

"Tim, let me ask you something."

"Sure."

The pastor handed him the pitcher full of water then grabbed a glass from the cupboard. Sara had finished the sandwich and put it on a plate. Gabe noticed she'd kept the ingredients sparse, probably knowing Gladys wouldn't want to eat much.

Gabe poured some of the lemonade into the glass Pastor Tim held out. "I'm not sure how to comfort Gladys right now. I mean, I'm still dealing with so much of my own stuff from my wife … my own grief. How can I comfort someone else?"

"Well, what would you want someone else to do for you?"

"I wanted to be left alone. I wanted to just fade away. To not exist anymore. I moved here to be ... well, to not be noticed. I wanted to wallow in my grief and live out my days alone."

"I don't want that, I can tell you for sure."

The trio turned to see Gladys standing in the doorway to the kitchen. Gabe felt his heart drop, feeling like he'd failed already at comforting his friend. Frozen in the spot, he waited for Gladys to say more.

"That for me?" she pointed to the sandwich Sara had put on a plate.

"Yes. Let's go out to the dining room. The boys made you lemonade too." Sara quickly ushered Gladys from the kitchen, and Tim followed with the glass.

Gladys's movements and the look of blank acceptance as she let herself be led pierced Gabe's heart. He couldn't do this. He couldn't be a comforter when his own heart was still broken. He suddenly felt lightheaded and couldn't gather a breath.

"I, uh, I need to go check on Daisy," he called to them. "I'll ... I'll open the shop until you're ready to deal with it, Gladys." He moved out of the kitchen and to the door. "Just, uh, just let me know when ... if you want to discuss ... you know, stuff." He turned and fled to the door.

He heard Tim call his name, but he didn't stop. Couldn't stop. He stumbled getting into his truck then backed out of the driveway with a screech. He gripped the steering wheel as he made his way back to his cold, lonely apartment. What was wrong with him? How pathetic. These people had done so much for him, and yet, he fled in her time of need.

After letting himself back into his apartment and calming down Daisy, he sulked to his bedroom, shut the door, and fell into bed fully clothed.

## Chapter Thirty-one

Gabe moved as if in a trance the next morning. The routine of his morning ticked by quickly. Before he knew it, he stood in the coffee shop making coffee and filling sugar. He liked routine. It helped him feel as though he had some control.

When the bell over the door chimed, he looked up with a forced smile, ready to greet the first customer of the day. But it was just Hattie.

She wore a more subdued palette than normal—dark green slacks and a light pink top. Her cane still sparkled from the sun coming through the side window.

"How's Gladys?" she asked as she toddled up to the counter.

"Fine. I mean, I guess. She seemed … tired." He didn't want to tell Hattie he'd fled at the first sight of his friend's grief. He hoped she'd just do her baking and leave him alone. That's all he ever wanted—to be left alone.

But Hattie pressed.

"We can head over later and give those church folks a rest." She moved to put on her apron, then took some muffins from the fridge and started arranging them on a pedestal.

Before Gabe could reply, customers began to come and go, and their morning fled. He wished they were this busy every day. Once more, he noticed no one bought breakfast sandwiches, but Hattie's baked goods were gone before eleven.

"I hope Gladys will feel up to baking again soon," said Hattie. "I'm worn slap out."

Gabe nodded, once again caught up in his own thoughts. He'd basically run out on Gladys last night. Perhaps she'd not want to see him at all. He wondered what would become of the coffee shop. Although only a part-time job for him, he felt comfortable here, and he had many memories of Bill here.

"Gabriel! Land sakes, child. Where did you go?"

He turned to Hattie and noticed her scowl, hands on hips. "I'm sorry. What did you say?"

"I asked if you thought we could close up early and go see Gladys?"

He didn't want to do either. "I think I'll stay open. Tuesday is usually busy here, people looking for new things to try." He could tell by the look on Hattie's face she was not buying his explanation. "Why don't you go and see Gladys? I'm sure she'd love that." He moved to wipe down the counter as another customer entered. He smiled and welcomed them, hoping Hattie would leave while he kept himself busy.

She did, and he felt a surge of relief as she walked out the door without a backward glance.

By one o'clock, Gabe had not had a customer in almost an hour and a half. He'd straightened and cleaned almost everything he could and closed the shop early for the day.

He'd gone upstairs and brought Daisy down for a potty break. She currently lazed in her bed in a patch of sunlight coming through a back window.

He sat in the plush chair normally reserved for Hattie. His thoughts were on Bill and Gladys, and the coffee shop, and what Gladys would do with it now that Bill was gone. He felt sure Gladys would want to close it down, especially since the business had proven to not be profitable. Gabe had pulled out some of the paperwork, hoping to make sense of some of it or to figure out a better solution for the business. He spread it out on the ottoman before him.

The first thing he noticed was the amount of supplies Bill ordered—seemingly way too many—and at such high prices. Perhaps Gabe could find better suppliers. He thought again about closing earlier as well to save on electricity. Maybe they could offer the space to groups in the evenings for a small fee. Perhaps Pastor Tim would know of a local Christian group in need of a space.

He made a note on a piece of paper he had nearby and then rifled through some other paperwork.

The baked goods were their best source of income right now. Gabe made a note to stop buying bread and other sandwich-making items. At least for the time being. Gladys would have to make the final call.

As he continued to ruminate over the business, a plan began to form. But he'd need to talk to Gladys about it. This was her business, and she'd have to make the final decisions.

Again, he wondered if she'd be willing. Perhaps this had been Bill's baby. What if Gladys didn't want to do anything but sell? Gabe thought about buying the business himself but was not sure he wanted to sink money into a failing business. He wasn't even sure what owning a business like this entailed.

He'd need to talk to Gladys.

Yet, he was not ready to see that lost look in her eyes again.

He pushed the papers back into an expandable folder and went to put it back into the office safe. This would all have to wait for now.

## Chapter Thirty-Two

A week passed in the same way. Gabe and Hattie opened the shop every day except Sunday. Gabe would spend those days at the beach mostly. Hattie prodded Gabe every day to go see Gladys, but he refused, always making one excuse or another. He knew he couldn't hold off either woman for long, but he wasn't ready.

He'd not ventured to church again, afraid to run into Gladys or more people encouraging him to see her. He knew he was being silly—his sister would say it was the grief directing him—but his stomach lurched every time he thought about seeing Gladys again.

He'd returned to his job at the Food Lion, confusing Brent and adding to his excuse of being busy.

He'd attended the graveside service for Bill, but from a distance. When the family had risen to end the funeral, Gabe had slipped away before anyone could approach him.

Now, as the last of the day's customers were served and walked out, Hattie had sunk down in her plush chair and said, "You ain't helpin' no one by avoiding Gladys. Haven't you figured that out yet?"

Gabe's mind was still on the last customer, who had ordered an elaborate drink. He was pretty sure he'd done it wrong. "What? I don't know what you're talking about."

"Gladys asked me how things here were going when I visited her yesterday. How you were." Hattie rubbed at her knees with the palm of her hand. "She's plumb worried about you."

Gabe looked up, startled. "How *I am*? Why would she be worried about that right now?"

Hattie shook her head and sat up straight in the chair. "She called you her son, you dolt. Remember that? She told them doctors and nurses you were her son, Gabriel. And not just to get you in the door. She and Bill love you like a son." She gestured with her cane in his direction. "That means something to folks like us. Why can't you get that through your thick skull?" Hattie rose on shaky legs and moved to his side. She poked him on the shoulder with one gnarled finger. "You idiot, she's grieving about *you* as much as she's grieving about Bill!"

Gabe took a step back, not understanding what she was saying. "I-I don't ... what?"

"She loves you like a son, Gabriel, a *son*. And she thinks—knows—you're hurting too. She's like a momma who wants to comfort you, but you've kept yourself so durn busy and separated from her ... she thinks you don't want to see her. She thinks you blame her for Bill's death."

Gabe's heart ached. He didn't want to see her, but not because of the things Gladys apparently thought. "That's not it at all. I can't deal with the grief. Not because of anything she did. I certainly don't blame her for anything."

Hattie waved him away and shuffled back to the chair. "She thinks she shouldn't have had Bill moved. That Outer Banks Hospital should have just cared for him. She thinks if they would have stayed there he'd still be alive."

"But that's not true!" Gabe came to stand next to Hattie's chair. "Outer Banks Hospital didn't have surgeons trained for the surgery. They had to move him. That's ridiculous."

*Changing Tides*

Hattie scowled up at him then. "Yep. Ridiculous. Just like thinking going to the store killed your wife."

Gabe gasped. How did Hattie know that bit of information?

"Your sister told me when she was here. Told me Ellie wanted to be home with you. Told me you dropped everything to care for her, including going to the store when she wanted something, anything." Hattie tapped his shoe with her cane. "Sugar, I bet she waited for you to go so she could slip away without you seeing. She knew. People *know*. She was hoping to save you some hurt, sugar."

Gabe stumbled backward into a chair and landed with an *oof*. That would have been just like Ellie, and it *was* a thought he had considered. But it didn't erase the ache in his chest that he hadn't been there with her at the last. And now he'd abandoned Gladys too.

Hattie squeezed his hand. She waited for a beat, but when Gabe remained quiet, she said, "Gladys needs you, Gabriel. And you need Gladys. Don't let the grief separate you from family."

Her words brought him back to reality. He'd vowed to God he'd stop doing that exact thing and yet he was still doing it—running, hiding from the grief.

And hurting another person in the process.

He stood. He needed to go see Gladys.

"Hattie, I think—"

Just then the back door swung open, and a familiar voice called, "Can I get a little help?"

## Chapter Thirty-three

Gabe rushed back to the door to see Gladys struggling to enter, a tray of freshly baked goods in her hands. He reached out to retrieve them from her, and she smiled as he did so.

"Thanks."

He nodded and moved to the kitchen to deposit the goodies.

He saw Hattie and Gladys embrace and speak in soft tones to one another before Hattie retrieved her cane and moved toward the door.

"I'll be back tomorrow, sugar. Think on what I said."

Gabe wanted to implore her to stay but knew he needed to face Gladys sometime. He should have gone to her, but now here she was. She'd moved to the table and taken a seat, waiting patiently for him to approach her.

"Sorry I didn't bring those this morning, but ... well, mornings are hard these days."

Gabe ignored her comment as he moved to stash the baked items on the counter, then wiped his sweating hands on a towel.

When he sat down beside Gladys, she took his hand and smiled. "I've missed you."

Gabe choked back a sob and pushed away tears. She needed him to be strong, but he was not sure he could be.

She squeezed his hand and then folded her hands on top of the table. "I know why you've stayed away, so I thought I'd come to you."

"I'm sorry. I just—"

She held up a hand to silence him. "Let me speak, please. I'm not here to punish you or make you feel guilty. I'm not even here to talk about Bill. Although, we can sometime if you want. And I'd like that." She glanced at him but kept going. "I'm here to talk about this business."

Gabe knew this moment would be coming, but he felt unprepared. He'd spent the last week devising a plan to keep the place open if Gladys chose to do so, but he felt almost certain she'd not want to. He took a deep breath as he waited for her next words.

"I'm giving you the business." When Gabe opened his mouth to protest, she held up her hand again. "Let me finish. I'm giving you the business ... if you want it. You can pay something if you wish, but I don't require it. You can turn around and just sell it, but I hope you won't. What I would like to ask is I can come and go still as I please and help now and again if I want. This place was Bill's dream, and I don't want to see it fail now. If you don't wish to take it over, I understand. I'll ask someone else. But I need to keep it going. For Bill."

Gabe knew exactly how she felt. Knew exactly what was going on in her brain. He'd done the same thing—lived his life for the last year for Ellie. But he couldn't let Gladys make the same mistake.

"No." When Gladys moved to rise, thinking the conversation over, he touched her arm, imploring her to sit back down. "I have a better solution. Hear me out."

Gladys frowned but sat back down, giving Gabe her full attention.

"We can add my name to the business, but we become partners." It was his turn to hold up a hand. "Listen, please. We become partners. I do all the books … all the running of the business, actually, unless you want some input. I'm happy to have it. But here are my suggestions.

"First, we're only open in the morning. Six to noon. Second, we don't serve breakfast sandwiches anymore. And we trim down the coffee selections."

"But if we close earlier and trim down the selections, won't we lose money?"

Gabe shook his head. "You'll save money on the supplies for the breakfast sandwiches we won't be making. We throw a lot of that stuff away anyhow. Most people only get coffee and a pastry. Which leads to my next idea."

Gladys raised her eyebrows, clearly interested.

"We refocus the primary point of the business."

"What do you mean? We couldn't be a coffee shop anymore?"

"Nope." He smiled. "The coffee shop would be secondary to your new business. A bakery."

Her eyes went wide, and she began to shake her head. "Oh no. I can't do all that at my age. I … I could never bake enough."

"We can use the ovens here. Hattie can help. I can help. We'll start small." Gabe knew this idea would work. Avon lacked a bakery, and most tourists wanted to eat sweets and live less healthy lives. He thought back to how Brent had mentioned tourists didn't come to the beach to eat healthy food. He was right.

"But we can offer gluten free things too. We always have folks coming in here asking for that. Or less sweet items too. It'll be a process, but I really think it will work."

Gladys put her hand to her mouth and looked away. Gabe couldn't tell if she thought he was crazy or if she was really contemplating the idea.

"We can invite book clubs or other groups for special events or something for the times we're closed too. With that space right up front." He nodded to the place where Hattie's chair and a few small tables sat. "I haven't thought all that out yet, and we'd need to do some trial runs, but basically rent out a small portion of the space for groups and charge a fee."

When Gladys still didn't respond, Gabe continued, "We need to ask the insurance company some things—to be sure we can do all this first. I haven't gotten to that step yet, but I've been thinking about this all week." Gabe hastened to add, "Or we can do whatever you think is best. I don't want to push you into something you're not—"

Gladys turned to him and said, "I want to be sure you're doing this for you and not just for me."

"Well," he said, "I want to honor Ellie's memory too, if it's all right with you. I want to have a small bookstore in that corner over there. We can lend or sell, maybe both." He looked at the wall where he thought a bookshelf might fit perfectly. He'd been thinking about this idea for the past few days.

She frowned. "You lived your whole married life to please Ellie. And I see how hard that's been on you now she's gone. But just doing what you think she'd want and planting me into the mix won't work in the long run. You need to know what you want to do and do that. If this isn't it ... I'd rather you not get my hopes up."

He sat back in his chair and thought for a moment. Is this what he truly wanted, or was he just trying to solve a problem like men do? He thought about going back to

Pennsylvania or Maryland or DC and shuddered. He couldn't. Too many reminders of Ellie … no, too much reminding him of what Ellie didn't want. The life she didn't want to live. Dreams unfulfilled.

Gabe took hold of Gladys's hand. "You're like my family. I have a life here … a pretty good one if I'd stop wallowing in my grief. Plus, my sister will be happy to visit me at the beach, so I'll probably see more of her and her husband. And there isn't anything left for me back in Pennsylvania. I can be of use here—that's what I truly need." He swallowed hard once. "Yes, Ellie would have loved owning a bookstore, but it's not just because of her that part of this idea came to mind. I found a bunch of my books in a box recently. I had forgotten how much I love to read, but I've been devouring them since I found them. There is nothing better than a cool bookstore. I want to offer the love of books to people."

"Does this mean you'll stay?" The pleading look in Gladys's eyes would have convinced him if he'd not already made his decision.

"Yes. I want to stay. I want us to work through these things together. I'm ready to move on with my life—which starts with you. But also honors Ellie and the things I love too."

Gladys threw her arms around Gabe's neck and cried into his shoulder. He felt his own tears swell and squeezed his eyes shut. They stayed that way for a time before she finally sat back.

"I'm sorry. I've been an emotional wreck this last week."

"As well you should. Your husband just died," he said softly. "Grief is natural."

Gladys offered a small smile and said, "I thought it would be easier this time around." She wiped her nose with a tissue. "When I lost my other husband, I had so much to do—kids to raise and a mortgage to pay. I kept going. I probably never grieved properly." She offered a small laugh then. "Guess it's all hitting me now."

"Yeah, sometimes it's like those waves out there on the beach. They just keep coming and hitting you over and over again—like grief."

Gladys nodded, but said, "I always compared the waves on the beach to God's love, not grief."

"I'm not sure what you mean. How are the waves like God's love?"

"They just keep coming, don't they? They never stop. Wave after wave of God's love. Sometimes soft and gentle, when we've pushed him away and he's trying to remind us how much he loves us, and sometimes hard and pounding, when we're being stubborn or forgetful about his promises."

Gabe thought about all the different analogies people have offered him in the last few weeks related to the ocean and its waves.

"I like that analogy. Thank you for that." Gabe put his arm around her shoulder. "And you have a lot of people who love you here too. I know Hattie would move heaven and earth for you. We'll help you through this."

Gladys leaned into his hug, putting her head on his shoulder. "And we want to love you as well. Promise to let us love you too?"

Gabe sighed. "I do. I've begun talking more with God. I'm ready for change. How about you?"

"I'm not ready to be without Bill, but I'm ready to keep moving forward with this business. When do we begin?"

## Chapter Thirty-four

**6 MONTHS LATER**

Gabe woke to his alarm going off. He slapped at the clock until the buzzing stopped, then wiped his hand over his face. He'd not slept until his alarm went off in so long, he'd almost forgotten what it sounded like.

When the work at the coffee shop had slowed during the holidays, Gabe had found himself sinking once more into a weird funk. He and Gladys had started to make preparations to change things over in the shop—ordering a new, larger oven and rearranging the kitchen a bit to accommodate her baking. They had begun offering more baked goods, which had been well received, even by the locals.

They'd rearranged a part of the front of the shop to set up some bookcases and to allow small groups space for meetings. Several clubs had begun meeting regularly and paying a small fee for the privilege. They had a small shelf of books for sale and a larger lending library for locals only. The books were especially profitable and fun for everyone. Hattie even held impromptu book readings for some of the children who visited the shop with their parents. Gabe could see her teacher mode switch into gear every time those little ones huddled up at her feet.

Gabe had decided to move closer to the beach, and they'd begun renovating the upstairs apartment for more space for events.

Tourist season had died down during the holidays, though, so they had decided to halt more change until it picked up again. Gabe had dealt with all the paperwork to amend the name to Beach Please Bakery, with Gladys and him as equal partners. Yet, he found he'd had time on his hands.

That's when he'd decided to finally go to the animal shelter and adopt a cat.

Daisy and Oreo lay next to him now in their own little pile. He smiled at how the two had become fast friends.

He'd seen the two-year-old feline almost immediately and been drawn to her. Black on her head and tail and white in the middle, he instantly knew he'd call her Oreo—like the cat he had as a child.

He scratched the cat's head, and she rolled over. He scrubbed her belly a bit before she curled into him and bit his knuckle.

"Enough love for one day, huh?" He laughed. Oreo liked attention, but not as much as Daisy. She was more solitary in nature, though she did allow Gabe to snuggle her from time to time.

Daisy peered at him with one half-opened eye, and he pet her head next. Suddenly, she leapt up, excited for their daily walk. Oreo stretched and snuggled deeper into the bed covers where Daisy had left a warm spot.

"I agree Oreo, but Daisy won't be ignored."

He rose and looked out the double sliding doors to the now rising sun. Since moving into his new home, a row

*Changing Tides*

back from the beachfront, he'd loved to watch the sun rise every morning. Each day the same and yet not. Each day something new. New colors, new timing ... always beautiful, even when rain loomed. He began to appreciate what Ellie had seen in the sunrise and sunsets every day. Watching them and truly appreciating them the way she did made him feel closer to her somehow.

Gabe grabbed a pair of sweatpants and a sweatshirt. Despite being this far south, March in the Outer Banks still rarely got above fifty degrees, and mornings were closer to low forties. But when he'd gone to visit his sister over Christmas, he'd practically frozen with the colder temperatures of Virginia. He marveled at how only a couple hundred miles could make such a difference.

He walked down the steps with Daisy in tow. When he opened the door to the outside, he spotted Hattie waiting for him at the bottom of his stairs.

The house he'd bought sat only two doors down from Hattie's—far enough that she couldn't spy on him. Or at least he hoped. But he didn't walk around naked outside just to be sure.

"Gonna be a cool one—you ready for it, sugar?" she asked as Daisy bounded to her. The dog sat dutifully, not jumping as she once had with the older woman. Hattie had trained her well.

"Where do you want to walk today?" Gabe snapped a leash on Daisy, and the two friends fell into step together.

"Let's mosey on down that side road that leads over the other development today. I think the Hendersons are doing some remodeling on that rental of theirs."

Gabe chuckled. Ever the snoop, Hattie made him think of Ellie's mom who had never missed a thing. As they walked, they chatted about other happenings going on and the upcoming tourist season.

"What's going on at the church these days?" Hattie asked. "The Christmas service was nice, but what do they do when it's not a religious holiday?"

"They have the whole Bible to talk about. You should really come more often, and then you would see. I really thought you were a church goer when we met. You know your Bible quite well."

"Eh." The clink of Hattie's cane punctuated her response. "The services are usually boring, and this old bird falls asleep too easily." But then, she smiled. "Maybe I'll come again for Easter. I do read my Bible, though. I'm no heathen."

Gabe laughed. He'd only just started really delving into church life again, but the people there had drawn him in—in a good way. He'd been afraid it would consume him as it once did when he and Ellie had served in their local church. But here it felt different. The church was bigger for one and had plenty of volunteers, so Gabe didn't feel pressured to help in every aspect. He'd been able to just be a member of the congregation. Plus, he'd started going to the grief group with Gladys. First, it had been to just get her started, but Pastor Tim's discussions had drawn Gabe in and helped him too.

"We serve a monthly meal for anyone who needs it," he told Hattie. "I plan to help with the next one, and so is Gladys. You could make some of your desserts."

"Gladys has desserts handled, I reckon." She glanced at him. "But I'll consider it."

They walked on a bit further, Daisy's nose against the ground every step of the way.

"Wonder what that nose knows," said Hattie.

"Anything and everything. Hey, speaking of meals, are you going to Gladys's this Saturday?"

"I think she invited pert near the entire town." Hattie laughed. "Not sure where we'll all sit."

Gabe laughed too. "Yes, I think Gladys wants to express her gratitude for everyone who has helped with the coffeehouse changeover and all the help the church gave for fixing up her house too. She didn't want to do it before the holidays because everyone had their own stuff going on or went out of town to visit family. But one of the church members offered some tables and chairs so I think we might try to sit outside."

"In this weather?" Hattie crossed her arms over her chest and shivered. "Guess I better bring my long underwear."

They walked a bit in silence, Daisy pulling at the leash, trying to sniff every tree, shrub, and patch of grass. When they came to the end of the road, Hattie pointed with her cane. "See? Adding another room it looks like. Guess they'll be able to charge more for the house and hold twice as many. Durn tourists will be crawling all over this place in a few weeks."

"I think it'll be more than a few weeks. Most people wait until about May."

Gabe looked at the house and thought the same but didn't feel the aversion to tourists he once had. Maybe he'd feel differently come next summer, but for now, he wondered if Nora would return. And even if she didn't, he felt excited for new groups of people who would come to enjoy their town.

*Their* town. He accepted this place as his own now. Even without Ellie, he'd begun to make a life here.

Hattie and he walked back down the road toward their homes.

"Let's head out to the beach today," Hattie suggested, grabbing hold of his elbow.

"Are you sure?" Gabe knew Hattie had trouble walking on the beach, but she nodded, and they began making their way up a path that led through a dune instead of over it.

As they came through to the other side, the beach stretched out before them.

"Tide's changing," Hattie said.

Gabe looked but couldn't discern any difference in the surf. "What do you mean?"

Hattie shrugged. "I envision the tides changing each season. They get stronger in winter, I think. Change their patterns. The water is colder, obviously, but also clearer. Now they're starting to settle down again." She shrugged. "Probably just my old fart brain. I could be completely delusional." She shuffled forward toward the water as Gabe watched.

He thought about her idea. He did think the tide was changing. And for the better.

The End

# Author's Note—Changing Tides

This story first came to me when I was vacationing in Avon, North Carolina, with my husband and friends. As my hubby and I walked one morning, we noticed locals going about their business. Kids got on school buses, and people opened their businesses for the day. We got to know a couple of local people that week, and my mind started to wonder what it would really be like to live at the beach.

The two main characters, Ellie and Gabe, are based on me and my husband. I've always wanted to move to warmer climes, but not necessarily the beach. My husband and I've talked about me dying first because my family has a history of dying young (although not as young as I've killed off Ellie). He has always asserted that he'd become a hermit and live out his life alone. I doubt he would, but the thought of that combined with this idea of living at the beach gave birth to my story.

I also wanted to dig into the way grief affects people differently. Some go on with life while trying to ignore it. Some make crazy, rash decisions—like quitting a well-paying job and moving to the beach—and some just fall into despair.

## Sue A. Fairchild

I've not had this kind of grief in my life—although I've lost my mom and grandparents, it's not quite the same as losing a spouse. When I think about losing my husband—God forbid—I think I wouldn't likely recover easily. He and I are so entwined it would be hard to find a new way forward.

This is what I chose to explore with Gabe's life. Like Gabe, my husband is a bit of a loner. He is a workaholic. He doesn't like people all that much—or so he claims. Yet, I see him interact with others in a way that says differently. He likes being around *certain* people. When those people are in his life, he has a spark to him. I think even though he might choose to be a hermit when I die, I don't think others will let him. And I think, in the end, he'll seek out someone.

All these musings shaped this story. I hope it helps someone with their grief—if only just to highlight the different ways we can each find to climb out from the pit.

# About the Author

**Sue A. Fairchild** has had many jobs, both creative (graphic designer) and not (insurance agent), but when she sold that first devotion in 2012, her whole life changed. Now she claims the titles of writer, editor, writing coach, webmistress, and speaker and has helped a variety of authors get their manuscripts into readers' hands. She loves working with clients who are working toward the greater good of sharing God's message in this world. And she hopes her stories do the same.

Visit Sue's website here:
https://sueafairchild.wordpress.com
The links to her books here:
https://sueafairchild.wordpress.com/social/
If you're an author, sign up for her free newsletter for writers
https://tinyurl.com/mrxb9fmf

Check out her YouTube page:
http://tinyurl.com/3p9x3su4

## Discussion Questions:

1. Have you ever experienced grief like Gabe has? As his life begins to unfold in chapter one, can you relate?
2. Gabe has chosen to start a new life in the Outer Banks after his wife's death. Do you think this is or is not a good choice?
3. At the beginning of the story, Gabe doesn't like Bill praying and doesn't want to discuss God. How does his viewpoint shift during the story? Why do you think it shifts the way it does?
4. When we first meet Hattie, she seems to be a bit of a curmudgeon. How did you feel about her by the end of the story?
5. Do you think Gabe's reaction to Bill taking him to a grief group is warranted or a result of his grief?
6. Multiple characters compare how grief feels with the tides. Which one stood out to you or felt the most impactful?
7. Do you think Gabe should pursue a romantic relationship with Nora?
8. Each character suffers from some form of grief. Which one do you most relate to and how does how they've handled it affect your own journey through grief?

9. Gabe finds it hard to connect to people in his new environment because he's afraid he'll be hurt again. Does the fear of being hurt prevent you from connecting? If so, how could you strive to overcome this fear? Do you think connection with others is important?
10. Elizabeth Kübler Ross wrote in her book *On Death and Dying* that grief could be divided into five stages—denial, anger, bargaining, depression, and acceptance. Can you identify any of those stages Gabe goes through in this book? How about the other characters?
11. How does Gabe change from the beginning of the book? Do you think he'll stay in Avon?

*Places to find grief support:*

**Support for men grieving a loss:**
National Widower's Organization—https://nationalwidowers.org/

**Support after the death of a child:**
The Compassionate Friends—https://www.compassionatefriends.org/find-support/

**Support for adults grieving a loss:**
Whatsyourgrief.org—https://whatsyourgrief.com/

**Support for grieving military survivors and families:**
Taps.org—https://www.taps.org/

**Support for the whole family:**
Pathways Center for Grief and Loss—https://www.hospiceandcommunitycare.org/grief-and-loss/

Also check with your local churches, Salvation Army, or American Red Cross for additional organizations, programs, and communities that serve those who are grieving.

**Coming soon**

*Changing Seasons*—read on for Chapter One

## Chapter One

Nora threw her bag down on the couch and walked to the fridge for a soda. It had been a long drive back from the Outer Banks, and she just wanted to crawl into bed and sleep. Maybe she could hold off returning to her real world for another few hours.

The sound of work boots pounding up the wooden front porch steps erased all hopes of that. The squeak of the screen door followed then more heavy footfalls through the house.

*How did he know I was home already?*

She turned with soda can in hand to look at her brother.

"Where have you been? You've been gone for a week."

"Is that how long it's been? Seemed shorter …" Nora popped the top of the can of soda and brought it to her mouth, relishing the ping of the fizz on her lip.

Dell stood with his hands on hips and glared, waiting for her real reply. They had played this game as kids too. As the slightly older sister, she often didn't answer him to his liking, but he would wait. He had that gift—the gift of patience. She didn't.

She sipped a drop of soda from the lid, then sighed. "Delbert Harper, don't get your knickers in a twist. I'm home now."

She knew he hated being called by his full, proper name—that was her gift ... cattiness and sarcasm. But she needed to establish the upper hand somehow as the older sister—she forty-four and he about to turn forty-one. Being away for the week had probably sent him into a tizzy. She probably should have told him she was going. Or where she was. And when she'd planned to be back. Or answered the multiple text messages he had sent her. Or answered his phone calls.

But that was all water under the bridge now.

"You're not funny, Nor. I thought you might be dead. You could've at least answered one text." Dell held up a finger to punctuate his point. "What do you think we thought?" The finger went back down, and he slapped his pant leg with the hand. "You could've been abducted for all I knew!"

Doubtful. No one wanted her that badly. Unless it was for work. Or to cast blame.

"I know Jill told you where I was."

Dell had begun to pace her hardwood floors now, the old wood shifting and creaking as he went. He ran a hand through his brown hair. Thinning, she noticed. Finally, he stopped to face her again.

"Life went on just the same this past week while you were gone, by the way. Not that you asked."

Ah, switching tactics.

"You didn't really give me the chance to ask, Dell." She pushed herself away from the counter and brushed past him back into the living room. "You came in here all hot and bothered before I even had a chance to catch my breath."

Her cottage was small but comfortable. Only one story and only five rooms, it had served her purposes for the past three years but now felt a little too claustrophobic with her brother breathing down her neck. Dell followed at her heels as she diverted out to the porch.

*Need some air.*

Dell followed her there too, the screen door slapping back into place behind him.

"And if it went on fine without me, what's the issue?" she called over her shoulder.

She went to the porch swing and sat with one leg tucked under herself. She took another sip of her soda—wishing it was mixed with something—as she looked out across the front lawn. Down the lane about a half mile was her brother's house, sitting next to her father's. But their father hadn't lived there for several weeks now. He lived with Dell and his family. Nora choked on the lump in her throat and took another sip of her soda to wash it away.

Dell paced the wooden porch floor in front of her now. "Daddy needs you. He's been asking about you all week, and I didn't know what to tell him."

A flush of guilt rose in her throat. She watched him pace for a beat, then said, "Dell, sit down before you give me a headache. I just had a very long car drive, and I don't need this right now."

Her brother glared at her once more before plopping down beside her. The swing bent and swayed with his weight, and she had to brace herself against the arm to keep from being toppled off.

"Well, since I had no idea where you were, I'm sorry I can't be more accommodating to your reentry into the real world." Dell pushed at the porch floor with one foot, setting the swing in motion.

"Jill did tell you, didn't she?" Nora turned to glare at him.

Dell glanced at her. "Yes." He blew out a burst of air from his mouth. "But Dad has been getting worse, and you just left me. And I'm handling all the stuff at the funeral home too. I needed to talk to you at the very least."

She could sense his frustration with her. But that was nothing new. He had always been the golden child. The heir apparent to their family's funeral business—even though she was the older child—just because he was a boy. She thought Dell resented her for that too.

And now Dell was taking care of more things—like moving their father into his home when he'd started to show signs of dementia. She'd been the one to run off when things had grown tougher, but it probably should have been Dell.

She also knew just running off had been the wrong thing to do, and yet ... she had needed to do it. And her time away in the Outer Banks had been a good one. Refreshing. Enlightening. She had even made a new friend. She sipped her soda and thought of Gabe, hoping he would respond when she texted him later. In fact, she should text him now, tell him she had returned home safely. Patting her pants pocket, she realized she'd left her phone inside. She didn't want Dell to linger, so she sat still, hoping he would get out his anger and return to his family so she could sleep.

"Jake has been looking for you too, ya know." Her brother looked over at her and she frowned.

She sighed. She'd texted him a few times, but only in short, vague ways.

They'd been on again off again in a committed relationship for many years, but she always ran from him. This time, they'd been planning their wedding. Again. This time, though, she'd agreed to a date in May. But as she'd begun to look at invitations and dresses, she'd felt sick. A queasiness she couldn't shake, until she'd run to the beach.

It wouldn't be the first time she'd called off a possible wedding with Jake. But they'd gotten back together so many times. Started over time and again. They'd first met in college.

Almost twenty years in the same relationship ... what was wrong with her? Why couldn't she commit? Jake had always wanted marriage, but Nora had wanted adventure. To get out of Millsburgh and see the world. He had seen part of the world and was not interested in seeing more. Millsburgh fit him like a glove, and he wanted to make it their home. Forever. Which made Nora feel trapped.

She knew she'd probably cancel their wedding again. Perhaps Jake would finally move on from her this time instead of trying to make it work. Maybe this would be his tipping point. She sipped again at her soda, again wishing it was something stronger.

Dell sighed beside her. "He thinks he did something wrong again ..."

*Nope. All me. Well, mostly.*

"... and wants to talk. You should give him the chance, Nor."

Nora turned on her brother then, all her calm melting like the last snow on the first warm spring day.

"Why exactly? I'm just not marriage material. I see that now. I can barely deal with the crazy inside my head. Why subject someone else to that for eternity? I can't even handle the family issues we have going on now." She blew out a hot breath. "I pick fights with him about everything. Always. And he didn't understand Dad moving in with you. He thought we should just put him in a home. Can you imagine?" She scoffed. "And if I'm going to have someone in my life, I want that someone to understand me and my family. To understand life is not just a big bowl of roses." She took a deep breath this time. "I don't even understand Dad's dementia so how could he? And I don't understand why I can't love Jake like he loves me either."

Life, in fact, had been pretty miserable this last year. She had gone a little bit crazy with all the things, in truth. It was one of the reasons she had wanted to get away for a bit. The other being to avoid Jake and their impending nuptials. When her friend Jill offered her beach house in the OBX as a place to get away, Nora didn't hesitate. She had packed her bags with the speed of a racing locomotive and left town before anyone could stop her.

"I had to get away. I know you don't understand. And I'm sorry I didn't let you know. Or Jake. I just needed to forget for a while. I needed to try and figure myself out." Her soda can now empty, she picked at the tab, making a pinging sound that rippled out into the late afternoon air.

Dell nodded. "I kind of figured that was what happened. Jill told me after a few days where you had gone. Made me promise not to come get you. Good thing North Carolina is quite the hike from Pennsylvania." He narrowed his eyes at her. "I wouldn't mind getting away too, ya know. Could have taken me with you."

Heat flushed her cheeks as she realized Dell was just as worn down as she. When their father's dementia had started a few years ago after their mother died, they never imagined it would get this hard. Now Dell had to work to keep up their family's business and two houses while his older sister just flitted away when things got too hard.

"So did you?"

Nora looked at her brother. "Did I what?"

"Figure yourself out."

She snorted. "Nope. Might be even more confused, in fact."

"Well, at least there was sun."

Dell set the swing into motion again, and a few minutes passed in silence.

When her thoughts began to get the best of her again as they often did, she asked, "Anyone die while I've been gone?"

Dead people wait, she knew, but families often didn't, and she was the face of Harper Funeral Home. She did the public relations bits—meeting with families, signing contracts, setting up obituaries, and running the actual funerals—while Dell did the behind-the-scenes stuff she couldn't stomach.

"You were lucky. Not a single one. Although old man Hoffmaster is supposedly not doing well."

"I'll call on his granddaughter Sarah tomorrow."

A few more moments passed in silence until Dell bumped her shoulder with his own.

"The kids missed you."

She arched an eyebrow at him. "But not you, huh?"

Dell smirked. "I missed all the things you do for the business. Does that count?"

"Nope."

"Well, then … Katie cried for almost two days straight thinking you would never come back. Feeling guilty yet?"

A little.

But she shook her head. "Nope. I needed to get away, Dell, and you will not guilt me into feeling otherwise." *I can do that well enough on my own.* "If you need to get away, I'll cover for you. For one week only." She put her index finger in his face.

He swatted her away and said, "Nah. I am a big, strong man. I no have feelings." He slouched like a caveman and scratched his protruding brow with a knuckle.

She poked him in the stomach, and he blew out a burst of air and laughed. Then he swung his arm over her shoulder and pulled her close.

"Yes, I missed you, you dumb bunny. And don't ever leave me again."

"Can't promise you anything."

He snorted, kissed the top of her head, then stood from the swing. "Welcome home. I have to get home for dinner. Natalie is probably worried sick. When I saw your car drive up the lane, I barreled out the door like a man on a mission. Surprised my phone's not ringing yet."

His words seemed to predict the future as his cell phone started to ring inside his pocket. Once more she thought of texting her new friend Gabe.

Why am I not thinking about texting Jake?

"You better get moving," she said.

He smiled, then stepped off the porch, avoiding all three steps. "If you need food, you know where to get some. Otherwise, I'll see you tomorrow. When there will still be food if you need it."

Tomorrow ... she didn't want to think about that yet.

To Be Continued ...

www.ingramcontent.com/pod-product-compliance
Ingram Content Group UK Ltd.
Pitfield, Milton Keynes, MK11 3LW, UK
UKHW020812280425
5656UKWH00033B/281